GREAT
AMERICAN
DESERT

STORIES

Terese Svoboda

MAD CREEK BOOKS, AN IMPRINT OF
THE OHIO STATE UNIVERSITY PRESS
COLUMBUS

Library of Congress Cataloging-in-Publication Data
Names: Svoboda, Terese, author.
Title: Great American desert : stories / Terese Svoboda.
Description: Columbus : Mad Creek Books, an imprint of The Ohio State
    University Press, [2019]
Identifiers: LCCN 2018043563 | ISBN 9780814255209 (pbk. ; alk. paper) |
    ISBN 0814255205 (pbk. ; alk. paper)
Subjects: LCSH: Short stories, American.
Classification: LCC PS3569.V6 G74 2019 | DDC 813/.54—dc23
LC record available at https://lccn.loc.gov/2018043563

Cover design by Nathan Putens
Text design by Juliet Williams
Type set in Adobe Sabon

CONTENTS

The West is a desert and we have been told
we would be wise to remember every moment
that roses also bloomed in Mesopotamia and
Syria and Tunis and Ur of Chaldees and
they are desert wastes now.

—Bernard DeVoto, 1948

CAMP CLOVIS

Summer camp, boys' footraces, showing off underwater, crafts with leather, spear point chiseling, campfires—the usual. Even Clovis boys camp, they get so troublesome in the village they are told to spend time elsewhere. Go roughhouse, they are told. Go work on your spear points and don't bother us. These boys would like to think this is just the usual, that they have moved their fires downriver because they always do, it's summer and that's when they're supposed to camp out. But this year there's so few kills at home their mothers pack no jerky, there's no mush and honey meal goodbye. Little food in the village means fights from who knows where, other hungry people, relatives or strangers—they will come at you. This makes everyone nervous. Stay out of the way, they are told.

Besides, they are supposed to watch the plants.

You don't send grown men to watch plants, not even a field full of strange plants. Plants just don't warrant the manpower. Women have to stay home to cook what there is, girls are all trouble. You send boys to camp beside the plants. The boys aren't going anywhere, they are going to camp anyway. It's summer.

These plants produce dreams. You eat one or two and wow. Then you retch, you have such a headache, your hands shake, but it's worth it. Nobody had ever even seen these plants until a season ago. Some who tried their seeds never came back from their dreams they are so good. Imagine, a whole year of dreams. But somebody has to take care of you when you dream, somebody points out. It's no picnic. And while you are dreaming, you can't fight, says another. All the others shrug and look forward to harvest, when the boys' guarding is over and the dreaming can start.

These boys are promised dream too by the end of the summer. If they're old enough to camp, they can dream. That's what their parents tell them. They don't have any ritual for these plants going yet. Maybe the plants come from the moon—look at the lines across the leaves, all ridged, says an old man. Everybody checks out the moon but few see a resemblance. They rip up a plant or two and inspect its root for moon-ishness and then burn it—ah, the scent, the promise of dream.

If only the plants could tell them where the game has gone.

One old man thinks there is no game because they ate the last bison. They haven't seen bison in three seasons, not since they ran that big herd over a cliff. The hunters deny that they took any more bison than usual, they say there are just fewer bison all around. Their wives spurn them. They love bison, cooked with sumpweed. The hunters retort that even the big deer is not rutting when it should. Maybe the deer have other wives, scoff their wives. The old man tries to suggest something spiritual is happening. The dancing leaves of the plant are like the fetlock of the bison and will lure them back, he says.

The wives say they see no game.

Spiritual or not, somebody has to watch these plants so they are not stolen or eaten by rats or coyotes or birds or die from drought. They are not game but maybe the boys will see game in their dreams and when they wake, they can go after them. Who better to guard them than these dreamy boys?

The boys are supposed to camp near the taller plants. Tassels have appeared along their stalks. Maybe hanging around the tassels will give them whiskers. Some of the younger boys have been pulling at the tassels with hope. The older boys say this plant will eat you if you don't watch out, then they say eating or smoking too much of this plant will kill you anyway. These boys don't like to sleep too near the plants and walk far away at nightfall to make their beds. These boys like to keep the younger ones up.

At least it's not some strange bird, says one of the younger ones. They watch a hawk circling what little stool the boys leave. Imagine a strange bird, with big leaf claws. He makes his fingers claws and caws, and the older boys laugh. Really, they all find the plants and their vigil ridiculous, unworthy of their freshening manhood. They scream taunts, they spear two-out-of-three, they make up silly fight songs by firelight, they whoop when they can't think of the words and fall laughing onto the ground, despite their hunger.

They dream already.

At night after everyone complains about how badly what little they catch is cooked—the hide slipped and the water seeped into it, or the rocks weren't hot enough when they dropped them in so the roots are still tough—one boy, the eldest, tells stories, ticking a hot coal with a bone, making it spark.

In the black of night when the stars of the stars hide under clouds and no moon at all shines, when you put your hand in front of you and you can't see which finger's the longest— several younger boys put their hands up to check—when the bugs go quiet all at once, even the frogs, other people creep up, he says. They have long hairy arms and strange eyes that catch the firelight. They will eat anything—his voice rises here—even their own children when they're slow—he smacks his lips—they are the ones who blow these plants ahead of them, blow the seeds with their mighty breaths—he puffs and puffs and the fire reddens—so they will eat our dreams too after they have feasted on us—one of the younger boys grabs for another, who screams—so you'd better watch out around those plants.

You're making it all up, pipes up a younger boy, once cross-legged, now crouched.

It's a story, he says, and the other older boys snicker. They are always telling stories and then saying, It's true.

Someone starts a chant, one of those mind-numbing repeats that goes on and on that charts everybody's parent's parents for six generations back. Quite a few of the boys join in, they like the sound of the chant, it's their sound, it makes them brave.

You're a liar, says the youngest after it's over.

The boy smiles. Few can see in this dark how the taunt gives him pleasure.

The next night the younger boys clamor for more stories, and the older one begins again. These hairy beasts have taken a liking for this place, he says. They have heard about it but have never seen it. Have you ever seen one of them in your dreams?

The boys say No, they have never seen them. Someone shakes his head *yes*.

If we take this place, say the hairy beasts, he says, we could be better than anyone else, even the Clovis. They have heard of the Clovis and their magic spears and their dreams, and they don't like what they hear. The Clovis are evil.

He opens his eyes so wide his whites gleam.

The boys object, they brandish their spears with their specially notched Clovis points, someone pokes someone else on purpose.

They challenge us to a running match and we beat them, suggests one of the younger ones.

I'd run to the end of the river, says the youngest of all.

You'd take a spear in your rear, says someone else.

Would not.

The story stops while the youngest wrestles the other. Sometimes the youngest wins these battles of his, that's what they wait for. Most of the time he doesn't because his toes turn in so his balance is off. Everyone yells over their fighting until somebody hears something growl beyond the firelight, then they all go quiet except for the two grunting boys who are rolling almost into the river, who turn on its gravel. *Hush!* call out two or three of the boys. Instead of quieting the wrestlers, the others join in—*Hush!* They go grave, hearing how quiet they can make this *Hush!* all of them together. Besides, there's no growling after they're finished, when the two boys, startled in the quiet, give up.

A storm sat on the land for forty days and the river began to walk, starts another boy.

What they like best is to throw mud at each other. Some of them stay mud-spattered for days, mud warriors, cool behind their mud shields. That is not to say they aren't drawn to the riverbank four or five times a day to churn it wild or douse their friends or just wade among the minnows in the shallows, shrieking about its cold. But after they don their shields, taking all morning to do it, letting one muddy coat dry before applying the next, the boys try to keep them on, strutting along the banks, dodging swipes from other boys or crouching, itching at the dirt caked to their chests. Sometimes they manage to keep their armor on for days, picking off the mud shards now and then and throwing them at each other.

The youngest has such a muddy behind, sitting bare-assed beside the riverbank, thinking about mud for pots and pots for food and his mother's food instead of a mud shield, thinking about the stuff they forage for themselves, boil up or roast in plugs of green or gray, and most of all, how cold the water must be, how he doesn't want to wash his behind but he almost wants to when another boy pushes him hard over the bank and into the water.

He squeals and flails his arms in the shock of the cold, he goes under, his legs rubber. He's spitting out water, he's clearing his eyes, he's wading out fast to get that boy who pushed him when he bumps a dead body sunk in the black of the middle of the river. On the bank, the boy who shoved him is hopping on one foot, hopping on the other, pointing at it. A swirl of river water curls out of the corpse's mouth as it bobs into the river's weeds. Neither of them think to retrieve it they are so shocked, then it catches in the brush, where the legs beat.

It's someone they know but there's so much water inside him, he's swollen into no one. Together the boys pull him out and turn him over and see the head wound, the stab in the side. Then another corpse floats up, and another. What? These are their villagers, the people who are supposed to protect them. The boys pull them out and then run, wordless, as quick as their fast legs and turned-in toes can go, away from the river, dodging the plants, fear moving from boy to boy back and forth, like a ball of mud. Where is everybody else?

When they're out of breath, which is not soon because they are always running, when the youngest falls too far behind and calls out, panting, to stop, when the question of cowardice seeps into their speed, they saunter up to the other boys play-fighting with their spears. These boys with their spears have fought so far and long that they've ended up where the plants show short in the horizon.

On the riverbank! the older of the two tells them, still out of breath. Come see! The youngest, still wet, pretends it's nothing so the older boys will know that it's really something.

The other boys gather themselves, they walk back slowly, listening to the boys' report. For real? someone says. Did you see anyone around? The boys say Nobody, they saw nobody else, the body was just there, and then the next and the next.

The bodies already stink from the hot sun when they return, the river water finished oozing from them. The boys walk around the bodies trying not to look at them, they look at the plants, at the river that brought them. This could be my uncle, someone decides at last, touching the swollen cold arm of one of them to make him real. One of the boys mentions wild dogs and they drag the bodies to the other side of the river, trying hard not to touch them too much, though they must.

Another body washes in, and a few parents. And a baby. They don't recognize the baby it is so badly beaten. Somebody's mother must've had it while they were gone, but the woman's body is the sister of someone else.

Even a baby.

They are just boys. They haven't seen death often, their families are healthy, the way most people are who live scattered. Grandparents have died, though some have not, some hold on like turtles. Someone's mother caught her foot between two rocks and a wildcat found her. No one says anything about her. Well, sometimes babies don't live, or don't live long. Adults should be here soon to explain, to take the bodies back, is what they decide. They don't want to send anybody to the village to ask what's wrong, they are not supposed to go back until the plants dry. They tell the eldest with all his stories to sit upriver, wait and keep watch for someone from the village. They move the bodies together, they decide to sleep close to them to keep dogs off.

The night passes with whimpers, with watching the plants against the stars, and the stars' glitter on the river, and, for a while, the big moon drowning in it. Nobody even lights a fire to roast the rabbit that hopped up in their quiet—someone might kill them too if their fire is spotted. The older boys join the younger in lean-tos they have to build from spears and hides, and they sleep.

By daylight only water has arrived. The eldest reports nothing more upriver. The bodies smell.

The boys row themselves alongside the river, squatting, waiting. None of them take their morning baths or roll mud to throw. The sun grows even warmer for this time of year, the smell worse. Someone gives out the rabbit someone else cooks in the bright light so the smoke disappears. Someone can't stop sobbing about his uncle. What about my father? sobs someone else.

They don't have anything to dig with other than their hands except for two sharp bones they found stuck in the bank that they've been using in battles, big bones of some animal they can't imagine, too big for even the elk that parade through their land once a year, bigger than the mammoth their fathers take down when they're very lucky, whose meat they like to dry into jerky. The boys use these huge bones to dig out the dirt to put over the corpses, digging stealthily, as if even the plants were watching, and pile rocks from the river on top of the dirt that covers the bodies.

They sit back quiet, resting. It is hard work, all that digging.

The youngest spots an antelope standing in the far distance. Antelopes are rare this season, or else hard to see if the grass is tall. He says they all should stay as still as the antelope, that is what he argues after it disappears. We should go nowhere the same way, pretend we are antelopes, blend in. If someone comes to kill us too, they won't be able to find us if we are that still.

They are coming for us?

They try to stay still but they are boys. The long hot afternoon is trying. They decide to run for as long as they can farther downriver, they decide No, they will leave this river and try to find another, they have heard of another in a song, the cranes often fly from there, they decide they must send someone back, they decide who.

The eldest and the second eldest. They give them the bone hook they found on one of the bodies so they will be believed by the village, they give them pale lumps of what food they have left, then they envy their exit, their doing something when they can do nothing but guard the plants.

Three days and their nights flow past those left behind, who try to stay up and not dream their fear too, they are afraid of sleep until a wash of exhaustion confuses all they remember, and they're overcome by a yawning desire to nap. Napping takes them elsewhere until they are blinking eyes-wide, unable to nap a minute longer because of their age and their vigor. They soon quarrel over what they saw in the river, little things at first, which bank the first body came closer to, which pouch held the bone hook. No one wants to dig up the bodies to check. The heat of the late summer makes them long to run into the distance just to feel wind against their sleepiness, makes them sick of each other, makes them less cautious. They want to shake the plants.

They peel back the fronds around the tassels, they sneeze. They hate to sneeze, it is as if they are obeying the plants, a kind of bowing, they hate it especially for having to watch them now when finding the bodies suggests they should be anywhere else. No one repeats the eldest's story about the strange people and the plants but they all remember it. Soon it is all they can do to keep each other from shredding the plants by the stalks, from ripping them up. They fall into fights over that, but silently, no one wants to admit their suspicion, their fear. There are dull thuds of fists on flesh, sometimes biting. They wish these plants would die. Some of the boys catch insects and let them crawl all over the plants. If the insects eat it, then it's not our fault if the plants die, is it? But none of the insects trouble the plants.

Someone sings old songs in the moonlight they wander in, and he sounds so sad everyone joins him. Instead of sleeping on full stomachs after their one meal at dusk, they chase each other in the dark until they fall to their knees, panting. They scream when one of them comes up out of the moonless black or someone nicks another with a spear he was just testing.

The two scouts don't return.

Days later, in the new light of a fresh morning, someone spots knots of green under the plants' tassels. If the insects don't eat them, says another, we shouldn't either. But by midday, someone has picked off one of the knots and sucked on it. Then someone else picks at them. No one should dream alone, he says. Both boys nibble more. The others stop rolling around in the dust, they end their games of straw and pebbles, and sing about death for these boys.

But the boys don't die. They smile. They say, You try some.

The boys don't eat it all. They have to save some for the village. Their mothers are supposed to come with baskets to lead them home, dancing and singing, with all that has been harvested. After that, only then can they dream. Even with the corpses and these two not returning? argue some of them.

They dream anyway. Someone says he sees a mountain fiery and empty at the same time, someone runs into a river screaming that the land is hot under his feet, he is burning, someone holds his ears from loud *booms*, someone wishes he hadn't taken his bite of the plant and rolls into a ball. Most of them dream in new colors.

After many hours their dreams stop and they vomit. They don't complain about vomiting or about what they dreamt. It is their own fault they sampled the plants. They would be cowards to complain, they would be cowards to return early to the village and abandon the plants. They don't want to be remembered for their stupidity either, what returning to their village altogether might also signal, along with cowardice. But they also don't mind not being remembered.

The next morning they poke each other, they feel better having dreamed the green off those plants.

When the plants' leaves begin to curl, they break camp. Their mothers haven't come with their baskets, the scouts never returned with news, but the boys can't keep waiting, they must go back. If there is food to be had at home, now is the time for it. They take their own time making up songs about how brave they are in the face of not knowing what they are returning to, they pack what few seeds and buds the plants can spare with the roots of some of the larger plants, they roll the dry leaves into long strips. Some sharpen sticks they find in amongst the plant stubble and pick rocks for their slings. Others stare into the stars or the sun with dread, twist their hair into knots and trail behind the rest. But none of them want to be left behind, with the dying plants and the buried dead, and none of them want to leave.

At the edge of the village sits a midden, a pile of heaped refuse every settlement builds, the trash of bones too tough or too big, the shells of river oyster, scraps of hide. It is not a tall pile—birds pick over it daily—but in this flat country, it makes a hill they can hide behind. They steal up to it in the dark and sit behind it silent, until one of the boys says it looks like those are someone's bones.

It's not a deer's bones.

Another boy says to shut up, you can't tell.

Leaving the midden, not quite fleeing it, they creep closer until they smell the stink of a meal that isn't theirs, hear no voices they know. They are hungry, they haven't eaten all along their river journey, they lean toward the smell, never mind the stink.

Then nobody's dogs attack, dogs that were once theirs.

They don't throw their spears—they don't want to lose them on the dogs, although the youngest does—an accident, he says later, and he's sorry, so sorry it was his toes he tripped on, while they hide in a gully not far away, shaking and furious. Men soon cordon off the starlight. They are not men that they know as fathers but strange men, not anyone who would be happy to see them, so many more men than they recognize, no wonder theirs are gone. These men herd them forward with their spears—worse, with the spear of the youngest, the one that he dropped, and the dogs try their best to bite them, their dogs now fierce beside the strange ones, their dogs who pretend not to know them.

The men wear hides that are not theirs, forked, in long loose skirts, although they notice one of them wears one of their father's capes. But that boy says nothing. The firelight in the settlement will soon enough show them everything's changed and none of them want that, none of them want to confront the nightmare of everyone gone, replaced by these new faces ghastly in strangeness. But the fire rises to a new-laid twig, and they see. Slant-eyed, with features flat and wide and bold as if stamped on and grown back harder, these people resemble no one they know, they are straight out of that made-up story. He dreamt them here, the eldest who is now nowhere. These people eat from bowls their mothers made, they eat and watch them, speaking to each other how? in what language? Listening, one of the boys accidentally leans into the stomach of the biggest boy and he pisses, he is that full of fear.

The plants save them. Everything they carry is taken and fingered and tossed away as trash until they unroll the leaves and the plant parts. Of course they recognize the leaves—it is the leaves of their plants. They want to know where these plants grow. That's not so hard to understand, language or no language. The boys think they will be killed after telling them where, so they stall and pretend not to understand. They go hungry for days, refusing to answer. When they are hungry enough, the boys lose their fear of one death or another, and lead the men upriver.

Slaves are what they become.

Later, it's only in the singing of certain songs that you can hear the boys' sorrow. After all, they saw none of the slaughter of their families, just a few corpses. It is as if they have been left behind and their families will return one day to tell them how far they have traveled, what fine meat they have brought them—although every so often, they glimpse a stone that someone's mother would never leave behind sewn into a woman's bodice—or was it hers? asks another. After they learn how to talk to their captors, they ask them if their families fought hard. They sat there dreaming, they say, from the seeds they had from the year before that they ate all of, knowing they would have more. They never lifted a club. Cowards? Some just fell into the river, they were that full of dream. But what about their wounds? What wounds? say their captors. There were no wounds.

One of the boys tries to ruin the plants that night and is whipped. Later the boys run upriver when no one is watching and pee into it, one after another, hoping to weaken the village with their waste. But the river moves too deep there to be caught by the girl filling her pot, or the boy lying beside the bank cupping his hands, or any of the women washing the babies.

Life is hard for anyone different. Years pass and there's only the youngest left, whom they treat as a clown with his turned-in toes, they throw scraps at his scrawny frame, laughing still at his every attempt to speak. When they want real fun, they hand him a spear to reenact giving away the other boys' hiding place. Still, when he finds a girl alone at the river, he wrestles with her and she follows him, despite her sisters' catcalls. Their boy flourishes, stronger for the struggle and born with good feet. When it's time to guard the plants, to fight off the rats and birds, coyote and wolf, he hikes to the camp with the others and is soon falling, laughing, into the river, shrieking into the hot breeze, crazy with the joy of summer, ready to dream.

But the river runs cloudy now. Even the banks have been planted.

MAJOR LONG
TALKS TO HIS HORSE

Major Long looks forward to mountains. Mountains he understands: rock, and streams that spring from snow, gentian and bellflowers atop green boulders at right angles, summits here and there, and tree-edged pools. This, he mutters to his horse, disappoints him.

Hand to brow, arm outstretched, pointer finger pointing, he feels his horse lift a leg in impatience. The horse is thirsty. Like himself and the other twenty riders, the horse wants to get on to water, dip its head into a stream and have it course down its impossibly long neck, its organs unshriveling. Yes, well, the view is not promising: first and foremost, no trees. If you need premonitions for your bodings, that lack says no to bodies of water, to underground seepage, to moisture anywhere that would attract a seed.

However, the grass here grows as high as your withers and not two days ago, the Pawnee had at least eight thousand ponies standing by. Then the head native put forward discouragement: If I even thought your hearts bad enough to take this land, I would not fear it, as I know there is not wood enough on it for the use of the whites.

Big Elk, that was his name. With regard to that *bad enough* insult, the Major's flag shows a scientist and an Indian shaking hands. Surely the elk man noticed it. Major Long is also quite proud of the steamboat it flew over, the first such vessel up the Missouri—he engineered its paddles himself. Was Big Elk alarmed by the boat's decorative elements? Painted with a gigantic black snake that belched the steam and smoke that powered the boat, its portholes bristled with guns, and the wheelhouse came armored. Alarm was the point. Surely what he meant was: Stay away from our gold. Anyway, that's what the military before him heard. Although no one had turned up much gold to justify all the torturing that so exhausted the soldiers, nor the lying these natives did to discourage the appropriation of their miserable land, or even of having three scientists and an artist along to memorialize Major Long's accomplishments—and where is that artist now, pray tell?

Major Long twists on his horse. The artist has his tools arrayed, and is duly filling the time and the sketch. The sentry tied him to his horse on account of his getting weak, and the charcoal and paper falling off at the least canter. He doesn't look that alert, although the doctor bled him profusely just after dawn, and he has refused to show his sketches for days. The Major is going to insist on seeing them, or stop his double rations, those that course through him so fast that administering them is a waste from the start.

Keep your eyes open, he commands the artist.

What do his sketches preserve anyway? Flat land, a bare rolling acreage like a poor muscle, and sand, brush in tufts here and there, mostly sky, and that is the end of it. Small game. One of the scientists decided the dog singing all night of their whereabouts was not a wolf but more of a jackal. No wonder it follows us. Snakes. He's seen deserts with fewer snakes that looked much more vicious than the ones in this part of the world. He turns his horse completely around for a new view of nothing. Steppes.

The guide says none of his people venture this way, he doesn't know the route through, and can he go home now? Sacred, he says next, or at least that's how the half-breed decides to translate him, whose father was a trapper who gave him away to the Pawnee along with a keg of brandy, a short-haired pale child, really almost a man, with eyes that shift from the guide to the Major as if between two thunderclouds. Sacred. Major Long has not been fooled into churches all his life to believe such a word. Being told he cannot pass is incitement, although he far prefers exploring mountains. He urges the expedition forward, On to the sacred!, but his horse refuses. He has to dismount and beat it. The legs of the beast shake but after he mounts again, the horse still does not walk. The others, by then, have traveled nearly a furlong ahead of him. They were perhaps annoyed by his discharging a pistol in the middle of the night as a way to test their coolness and self-possession. He suggested that they had eaten too many currants the night before, and that was why they were so loathe to rise. Look at how many miles they have gone already today! And certain of their coolness, and no more currants.

The horse, after a drink from his canteen, moves on.

Thus Major Long explores under the hot and harsh light of this world. It is never spring or cool autumn when he leads expeditions. It snows heavily on mountain passes and rains at every swollen river, or so it seems to Major Long. Climate is cruel, that is the lesson. He shares this observation with his horse, who shakes its tatty mane. He does not put this in his report, taken down daily by his aide-de-camp, a dolt whose love he writes to every evening as if he had only a few hours left of his life and will recount them in excruciating detail until he falls asleep and rises the next morning with less dread. Perhaps he too is intending to publish.

The doctor tells me that walking will improve your health, he says to the artist, as soon as he catches up.

I don't want to walk, says the artist. I can't.

Major Long raises his plumed hat. He's just had it replumed. He means the raising as a signal of his disapproval of weakness. Nonsense, it says.

He rides forward. Constitutions are all that matters in leadership, he says to his horse. His country has one, and his own fits that one perfectly. Men have rights so long as they are strong enough to exercise them.

Without warning, the sky goes dark and storm clouds cathedral-high roll toward them faster than the men can curse them. The artist had taken sick in a storm in the first place, painting in the rain, and stood so wet afterwards steam rose from his clothing beside the fire. Get that man under the tent, Major Long tells his aide-de-camp. The soldiers are busy tying up the horses, one or two having fallen to their knees for lack of water, and the scientists are stretching out canvas to catch whatever rain might fall.

The artist creeps under the downed canvas with his tools. The rest of them stand in the rain, tongues out.

Soon the guide perishes, of what no one knows. It is, after all, his land, and surely he is suited to it. It is also noted by the aide-de-camp that the half-breed's eye has started to wander in his head, giving him a crazed look. The boy makes no secret that he does not want to die like the native, exploring. Major Long no longer trusts him as a translator. He follows the sun.

They meet a rise and take it. At its bottom, his horse begins to paw the ground. As much as Major Long digs his spurs into his flank, the horse again will not go forward. He swings his legs off in fury and loads his gun and shoots the animal. The soldiers drag off the load and butcher the horse, catching as much of the blood as they can. They are all ready to remount when the artist walks up to the Major with a sketch. There, he says, and thrusts it in front of the Major's pince-nez.

Major Long says he can see nothing, just a dark patch in the middle of light.

It was wet, says the artist. Under where the horse deliberated.

The others look off into the clouds.

Are you telling me that the horse found water?

The artist shrugs, and in retaliation, the Major takes the artist's nag. The artist will walk at last.

Major Long is soon pointing ahead again, his skinny forefinger burnt from gunpowder, his nose red from the sun, his dress hat collapsed and his ears still quite deaf from the shot. Innumerable buffalo have the temerity to appear at a distance just as he is solving the problem of the design of a steam carriage. Link them together! he shouts to his horse.

Perhaps the approaching buffalo inspire him. They swirl past, parting at his scent, closing in as they proceed. Befouled dust blinds and chokes him, swarms of gnats and flies are drawn along in the swirl, and the rush of these moving thousands sting and buzz at his eyes, ears, and nostrils. After a few long hellish minutes, the herd veers and only the sick and young totter behind, calling out for the rest.

All the men survive, though the insect specimens, pinned flat and desiccated, whirl off into the unknown. Even the artist's work, rolled in a cylinder, is intact, though the artist, on foot, suffers a broken shoulder and the loss of most of his clothes.

That evening, mumbling at the campfire because the new horse doesn't seem to hear him, Major Long works on his report. Do these buffalo drink from some mammoth underground cave full of water? And what of the grasses, how can they flourish in the poor sandy soil without moisture to wet their roots? He comments to the aide-de-camp that every drop of that torrential downpour was gone in an hour. The dolt replies that sand has a way with water and swallows it like wine, and dolefully holds out his cup.

The wine was drunk fifteen days ago, all except his own. He has had enough of the trip. He tells the aide-de-camp to label the map *Great American Desert*. The expedition had not been his first choice, the insect man is despondent, the aide-de-camp's hat has been trampled, the artist has run out of blue and is now complaining about his shoulder, and the botanist is bored to madness.

Not a mountain in sight.

DUTCH JOE

Lands sakes is what we're always exclaiming because land is all we're good for, all the sakes there is or ever will be. Each of us, fifty or so strong, have fled a country crowded with kin or else lorded over, every inch of the land spoken for down to the last hop of hare, or squawk of fowl. We settlers have pushed all the way into the pockets of Lady America, hoping to take her wealth for ours, her endless waving grain and her cattle in abundant herds. Through our boot soles, thin as they are, we perceive the urgency of the land's fecundity to be ours, it is so empty and waiting. Even the clouds suspended above us are our clouds, borne in the reflection of our great desire. We slake our thirst for our own land by possessing Lady America with the plow. We are homesteaders.

Water is our first necessity and our greatest difficulty. "Great American Desert" is how Major Long chose to mark where we have come to settle. The hills of this desert roll, there are gullies, draws, washes, and gulches enough, but few rivers to plant beside. The Dismal River, missed by Long and named wrongly from our point of view because we celebrate any appearance of water here, is the font of our livelihood. We have to whip our horses away from this river to the plat we have staked out miles away.

The Indians tell us that any animal that has wandered too far beyond the river is counted as dead by them. However, we are not too sure about trusting Indians about where to settle or where the water is, given that we are removing them. When a man tells us he saw a cow wander back from this desert with a calf, and they stopped at a sandy incline not so far away and hoofed at a hole that water filled, we run with our shovels and picks and start digging. But where is that water? We dig very deep, two hundred feet or more, shoring up the sides of the well with the buckboards of our wagons as quick as we can build a dugout to shelter us, then we have to send for cedar for more shoaling. We do this work after we plow our share of the land near the river, after we seed it, after we pull out the weeds, hunt for meat, collect dung for our hearth, and haul buckets of water from the Dismal for cooking. We take turns digging this well whenever we have two minutes put together. It's not bad digging through the sandy topsoil, but there's rock after that, dry hard rock that blunts the shovel and our strength. We soon build a teepee of wood at the top of the well to lower down a bucket and a man. But all we get after all that digging is the dark cool of a deep hole.

We try again with another hole. We have to. The clouds seldom clump and darken overhead, they scud and thin and do not bless us. The Dismal becomes itself, dismal, it narrows, it slows. We get worn out digging and having to walk our teams so far from the river to tend our crops and we get thirsty, and our horses and mules drink themselves swollen as soon as they return. We grow weary without more water, and will be weary until death without it. The Dismal turns itself into slurry. Our crops will soon crisp and ash before we can harvest them. These few rains that wrung themselves out of the clouds when we first came, haven't come again. It just isn't the land for farming, never was: the broadsides sold us a farmer's dream. We shrug when someone says this, we sight down from our bad well to where the land creases into a gully and we dig another one, closer to the middle of the land we're trying to hold onto.

This third well isn't as deep as the first, the sides of this well are not as neat, they're a bit crooked and probably dangerous, which makes us want to give up on it even earlier. We have to dig through and after harvest to get that far, before the ground freezes and the snow fills it. We take turns digging inside it at high noon when it's hot, then we nap at the top before going back to our fields, then we go back down after work until dark, and emerge discouraged. What else can we do? The Widow McNash says she'll have her children try digging, there's got to be water, and sends one monkey after another to the bottom of the pit, until they dig down to forty feet and catch the cough.

That's our last try. We seal the hole with boards for the winter, our heads bowed, pounding those boards tight.

Then Dutch Joe shows up on a buckboard. He is a sturdy fellow of medium height, a pleasant smile, determined lips, and extraordinary muscles. I call him brave as well, this man in the tintype I still have in my parlor as a remembrance. He's holding a chair back in it like somebody dared him to, with one arm akimbo, and all his great muscles hide under a button-to-the-neck jacket, with boots to the knee and some type of Dutch flat hat crossing his forehead. In the tintype you can't see his bravery but you couldn't see him working either—he was always underground, always digging.

At first nobody thinks much of Dutch Joe's digging ability. He doesn't say anything to flimflam them, he just sees the piles of dirt beside the hole we gave up on and says he can help. He says he gets his digging power from the Dutch dikes he had to maintain for his father when he was a boy. He says every Dutch boy knows the power of a shovel or he drowns finding out, and he knows where water is hid from his home efforts. Here, instead of piling dirt up to keep the water away like the Dutch have to, he will pile it up to find it. This upside-down proposition pleases him no end but nobody takes him up on it. A lot of fellows tell Dutch Joe to get lost or if he wants to so much, to dig a well by himself. But if he digs for himself while everybody else is plowing, Dutch Joe says, what will he get for his own land? He must be paid by their labor on his stake. He who doesn't find himself important, isn't doing his job, Dutch Joe says.

While I'm cleaning my boots of dung dropped from my horse that I follow all summer, Dutch Joe tells me a story about the snakes in Sumatra, where he soldiered for a short time on behalf of his country, snakes, he says, that will come at you out of the trees. He likes the land here since it has no trees on it. The only snakes here live in holes, he says, sluicing a cool drink out of the river. Or they are those who don't believe I know where to dig.

I like Dutch Joe's confidence, it is just what the land needs. I give him my shovel, the one I brought from Pennsylvania with the maker's mark on it. I promise to plow and to plant for him if he will do as he boasts, produce water. If he doesn't, he will give me half his harvest that I put in the ground. He walks from end to end of my land, then takes off for a hillside that looks like all the others and starts in digging. Everyone laughs at him, they do laugh from that first shovelful onward, but not me. I am plowing for him, I don't have time to laugh.

An orphan boy works with him. He runs the winch and bucket and lolls about in between. He knows Dutch from his parents, who hid him inside a pickle barrel from Indians they should not have met. They believed that Indians hated pickles and the smell of brine burning, and he is proof that this is so, the Indians did not burn the barrel but all the rest and the parents too. The orphan boy gets a rescue from a wagon train that plans to hand him off as a go-back. He is already here, Dutch Joe argued and they let him stay with him because they could talk to each other. The boy is intent on growing despite his scare in the pickle barrel, and Dutch Joe feeds him well. Dutch Joe also tries to teach him lessons about digging. What the peasant doesn't know, he doesn't eat, he says, and the boy is grateful.

Every night the boy winches Dutch Joe up to land where-upon Dutch Joe loads my dirty shovel onto his shoulder, tips his beret low over his eye as if the setting sun is still too bright to see, stretches his big muscles in every direction, and walks to my wagon for sarsaparilla, a brew that's worth the roots you have to pull for each batch. The orphan boy tidies the pile he and Dutch Joe have made of the dirt all day, then follows along.

Drinking my drink, Dutch Joe tells me more about the snakes in Sumatra and how they spit, and asks about the rattler nests he's heard he will come across underground but hasn't yet, says that he'll shovel these American snakes away, and keep on shoveling past them. It's dark in the middle of the day at the bottom of the well, he tells me, about the same darkness that the jungles in Sumatra have from growing so many trees up against the sun. He tells me about the birds there that are striped like a tiger so you can't tell them apart from the tigers that hang in the trees. The thing he likes to tell best is about the stars at the bottom of the well he sees when he digs really deep, stars that shine at the top even during the day. You go down far enough, he says, fifty feet and more, and when you look up to waggle the bucket, there's the Milky Way and the Archer. The Archer gets brighter as I dig deeper, it's how I measure my going-along straight. Then he's asleep on his pins and the orphan boy and I lever his legs up on our bench for the night.

The orphan boy soon has a frame built over the hole and is shoveling a berm around it so no one falls into it or kicks in a rock while coming to view its wondrous depths. I am proud when my neighbors gather to spit beside it because it is so deep, and my daughter even walks all the way out to inspect it. Soon she is bringing sewing and sits beside the orphan boy while he flexes his muscles over the bucket-lifting. I wave at her when I pass the dig with my horse, plowing and seeding. My wife stays behind, under our lean-to, ailing. She wants to move away from the river and have her own place with water, she says then she would feel better, which is the best reason I have for taking the chance with Dutch Joe's digging. She hopes, like I do, he's working the right spot.

Water tells you where it is in many ways, Dutch Joe says when I review the fruit of his labors. He unhooks the harness he uses to lower himself down with and fishes a couple of arrowheads out of his pocket, the kind Indians are still making to kill us with, and a piece of a pot they must have broken a long time ago, judging from how deep it was where he found it. These people leave their things where you would after you toss them down, he says. They help me know where to dig, he says, and I half believe him. The orphan boy says he has never failed in his well digging, but he is loyal and should be.

Dry enough for you? the other settlers say to the Dutchman when he brushes his clothes free of dust on Sundays. They're looking for nails at low tide, he says instead. I try not to feel the fool for hiring him. I plow and I plant his seed and mine, all the time waiting, all the time bringing water for my wife from the river where she sits on a rug beside the wagon wheels, the only part of the wagon that isn't holding back the sides of the well.

One night I tell my own story to him and his orphan boy. I was a tradesman in Scotland, I say. I read the papers and spoke to many important folk, maybe one too many because one of them convinced me to close down my shop and come here.

My daughter doesn't quite laugh, my wife pokes her with a stick.

Joe tells us the circus strongman, Belzoni, dug into the pyramids of Egypt and found chambers connecting the dead wrapped up in rags. You will not find such things ever if you are having to tend a shop.

I relight his pipe.

Also, Joe says, puffing, I have it on good authority that you can tell the future by looking up from those holes. It has to do with those stars you see that way. But you don't want to look up too often. If the sky comes down, we'll all be wearing a blue cap.

I pull off my cap and scratch my bald head and he laughs.

I loan the orphan boy the use of my rake and he spreads the loose dirt they have made and sows it with rye, a crop that grows fine here, that doesn't need so much water. He and my daughter, who is weaving and sewing a blanket out of empty seed sacks, sit together on that hill after the rye gets some height on it, whenever the boy is not switching out buckets and mending rope. When I bring my daughter and him a cup of water from the river, he says Dutch Joe will make everyone rich as soon as he finds the water here. He says he heard Joe once hauled a bucket of it out of a desert. I don't know about that, I tell him the next time I swing the horse around. But the pyramids got built and if there's any future in water a desert is where it would be, one of those oases.

We are pulling up the rye around the hole, the boy and I, it is that late in the year for the harvest, when we hear *Nou breekt mijn klomp!* from far down in the well. That breaks my wooden shoe is what he's saying, says the boy, stopping his work. I brush the chaff off my front while he peers over the well's edge to hear more, then he laughs and hauls up a clattering bucket.

It's wet, this bucket, it's full to the brim with water.

What a celebration! I run most of way back to the settlement for whatever naysaying homesteaders might be loitering, for them to come for a drink of my fine well water, all along the way shouting to the other settlers off in the distance. By the time I return, Dutch Joe is unharnessed and lies gasping on the ground beside the bucket, muddy all over.

My wife, sick as she is, rolls out a pie that night, fills it with dry cactus fruit and cooks it in a pot hanging over burning cow chips. It cooks slow and hot and long and the pie turns right sweet enough for Joe and his orphan boy and all the rest of us. We drink sarsaparilla aplenty and dance to the comb-and-saw players that collect.

Dutch Joe has the customers lining up.

He digs large, round cylinders, straight as a gun barrel from the grama grass roots to the gravel underflow. The settlers break out more new prairie for him, do all his farm work, and order him fence posts from the East to hold back the well walls. Myself, I give him the rye field in extra payment so I can hear his stories more often—and for another reason. His orphan boy has a boy of his own by then, named after me. My daughter spent too long on her blanket behind the rye with him, and myself one too many turns away from the well. The windmill doesn't care for wind that's gone past, says Dutch Joe, which I take to be his way of talking about spilt milk. Their engagement is short but my daughter doesn't cry on my shoulder, not even after her mother dies, the new baby boy in her arms. The baby has come just in time. The orphan boy and Dutch Joe visit as often as they can, and have their picture taken when they can't so my grandson can see his Pa whenever he wants.

Dutch Joe just liked his picture took and you can tell that from the one I keep.

In seven years Dutch Joe digs over six thousand feet of well, sometimes as far down as two hundred sixty feet, sometimes down ten feet, and not a one of them is dry. When the orphan boy and Dutch Joe take a day off, they run footraces with my grandson in the dark after dinner is finished. Winded, Dutch Joe smokes a pipe beside my fire and puts his hand on the little boy's head and talks of the future. He says the future he sees from the wells is all a-glitter, the stars bouncing their light off what the worm leaves in the dirt. Boy, he says to the orphan boy, you think of a way to elevate the water so you won't have to do all this digging. I will put myself out of a job, the orphan boy boasts. But what Dutch Joe finds is not an underground river you could sail a boat across into Hades but trapped water up to nothing in the rock and dirt, or so he says, if I got it right, his Dutch talk thick when he and the boy sit together. At the bottom of that last well, Dutch Joe says he saw a machine going across the sky as silver as a bullet. The orphan boy believes him.

It rains buckets in '91 and burns in '94, burns so bad men and their families pick up the bleached bones of starved animals to grind for feed. The paper says the building and operation of the railroads and telegraph lines generally precede a steady increase in rainfall since the electric current disturbs the atmosphere, and so does the rushing of trains. We don't yet have the railroad or the telegraph or a train so we will have to wait. Heavy rainfall also follows artillery battles as a result of the detonations of guns but nobody has the interest or the energy to fight each other here. Even the Indians have moved on. When the rain stops for good and the land shakes itself off with the wind, nothing we plant holds. Some days even my well is dry and the Dismal has gone muddy and is nearly gone. We will have to give it up too if Dutch Joe can't find more water. Others want theirs dug again too but I am first since I was first before.

My daughter sits beside the orphan boy while he works the bucket, happy to resume her post from so long ago. She dislikes the lonely place she cooks in, so far away from him. They build a shelter from the sun for the boy and he digs his holes beside them in the new dirt and elsewhere, when he doesn't have chores they think up. She is feeding her husband the trimmings of her pastry or maybe the sugar lumps their boy doesn't get all of, and is talking on about the boy's clever ways with a rabbit snare when the steel catch that holds the bucket somehow slips. The bucket is near the top and when it is released it falls directly onto the head of Dutch Joe working two hundred feet down. The orphan boy screams *Dutch!* and then *Dutch!* again, louder. There is no sound I imagine as bad as that bucket coming up. Get help, he says to my daughter, and he stares down into the well and stays there until I come running.

He don't look dead to me, he says before I peer down and see what he's been looking so hard at, Dutch Joe slumped against one wall.

I don't know what to do but nod.

A grown man can't maneuver in the bottom in rescue with another man in the well. My grandson has to go down. The orphan boy puts him in the bucket himself and doesn't answer his boy's cries until he can't hear them anymore. But the boy does his duty and ties the rope to Dutch Joe's harness, and the orphan boy cranks the bucket up with his boy inside and Joe harnessed below it, his muddy head wrong. At the top the boy leaps out of the bucket into his mother's arms and the orphan boy and I lay Joe beside his hole.

Men who risk their lives on battlefields are called heroes. Those who risk them in the construction of homesteads in such a desert as we have are also heroes. Let no one who has never dug in the darkness and the danger of a deep well dispute it. Among these heroes I write the name of Joseph Crewe. We clean him up for his coffin but his boots are worn thin and fall apart. We give him a blanket to cover his feet, and the shine of the worn coat we unearth from his chest. We come to find out from what else is inside that chest that he left behind no mule nor child nor wife anywhere.

He gave us life.

The orphan boy goes to work on the well himself and we are saved but my grandson doesn't go near the well ever again, won't haul up a single bucket's worth no matter what he's promised. I seen those stars, the boy says. It was night too soon.

DIRTY THIRTIES

Peel these couple of potatoes and make the pig happy, her sister says. It's been eating dirt.

Molly gets taken by the arm into the kitchen, Molly looking right past her—she is the shorter sister—right past her ear. You see another duster? says her sister. That spread of cloud isn't a thing to worry over.

She gives Molly the peeler to grip. Molly takes up a potato in such a way as to break your heart, like it was left alone in the bin. Which it almost is.

Her sister goes about her business, ripping feed sacks into strips. She has been up to this since early morning, since she saw her head-shape in dust around her pillow. She has seen that before, when she was sure no weather like this could go on and on, and she didn't fuss with caulking the windows with feed sack. She's going to fuss now. She was never so careful a cleaner as Molly, Molly used to sweep at the dust in the middle of the night.

She steps out to the barn to get another sack to rip and returns quick.

The kitchen's empty. She throws down her burden, she wipes her hands on her bum. Molly!

Where she finds her, this time in the bedroom, Molly's face is wet, teared-up. The pump's about dry out there and you've got it spurting, says her sister. She drags her back into the kitchen. She finishes the potatoes herself with Molly looking on, Molly looking on and on. You got to keep busy, she says. She gives her the scrub brush.

Molly sinks to her knees. There is hardly room for both women in the kitchen and Molly works wide, will scrub out a whole corner in a single swath. Her sister splashes down some dishwater and Molly scrubs and scrubs, then sits back on her haunches and looks toward the bedroom and coughs.

You catch that dust cough now? Her sister pours milk into a cup and gives it to her. Tastes like tumbleweed, she says. Cow doesn't eat anything else.

Molly stares into the cup. Slowly she drinks it.

Her sister starts ripping the strips of feed sack again, humming what song she heard on the neighbor's radio. Car coming, she says after a bit.

Molly's already half-legged it back to the bedroom. Her sister doesn't aim to stop her, she hasn't the heart for it, she knows who's coming too.

The old young man drags in, his britches gone to thread and his head low. Molly any better?

She's in the room, she says.

He takes a seat on a turned-around spindle-back chair. Well? Get her out.

You do it.

He does not so much as move a muscle.

Molly, come on, she says. He's here. He's tired of coming.

She has to pull her out this time, pry her fingers free of the door frame, then she forces her to sit beside him at the table that he's pulled the chair to.

Molly coughs.

Honey. He takes her hand.

I kept her in the house all day today, her sister says. It's not so far to the road that if she'd run, with her luck, there'd be a car coming. There are more cars today, going away.

Molly turns his hand over and touches where it is lined with dirt. The baby, she says, quiet as if it will wake.

He flips his hand and holds hers down so she can't get away. He heaves a sad sigh and sticks his head even with Molly's so as to look her in the eye.

Molly breathes heavy as if her stomach's about to turn.

After a while of watching the two of them, her sister says, You got to try to work the plow again. We can't eat a plow.

He drops Molly's hand, runs his own through his hair, says, Another duster coming.

You're as bad as her.

She takes things out of the cupboards they're kept in, flour goes in a cup, she ladles water into it.

He watches her as if he's out of practice looking, then he looks into Molly's face again, where it is crossed with dirty tears, then he stops. Sawyer said he found his way back to his house today only because his fence was glowing like a light bulb.

You don't say, her sister says. She has a paste of flour and water going.

Some kind of electricity that comes with the dust. Lit it right up, made the fence come alive.

Molly starts—what does she hear? *Alive?* She wrenches free and gets up out of her chair and takes a step for the door of the bedroom.

Dead is dead. She knows it, says the man.

Molly has her back to them, she's dragging herself almost to the threshold.

Her sister says, Cold for July, and shifts the cup toward the window where a single cloud sits over by where they once wanted to put in a big new street, or so she says, and then goes on: Old man Dickens walked all the way over here to give me these feed sacks.

Nice of him, he says.

Molly has slipped out of the room.

Her sister slathers a strip of sack with the flour paste, her hand running it the whole length.

He watches her. I tore up the cover, he said, yesterday. Before the storm. Just before.

The cover? The bed cover?

I mean—he puts his hands to his eyes and rubs—I mean land cover. I did plow, and the land pulled back as nice as a piece of cake. It would've grown corn, it was that kind of dirt. I plowed it and it come up and then the wind blew it away like it was waiting for me to get a mouthful of it.

He scratches at his stiff hair. I want the flour sifter if you can spare it.

No, she says.

After Sawyer told me about the electrified fence, he showed me an arrowhead the size of a knife blade. Yea size, he says, his hands wide. He said he took a flour sifter down to his blowout and found it. It's worth money.

Not with a sifter did he find something as big as that. You find it yourself with your eyes.

I ain't got the knack, he says, looking hard at her.

She wipes the paste off her finger and goes in and brings Molly back into the kitchen, gets her set up with her scrub brush again. Molly scrubs out a new corner, moving the dust and water in dark swirls. Maybe if she were expecting again, her sister says. Maybe that would perk her up.

The man slaps his thigh, and dust from his pants rises into the air. I don't know how that will happen. You know she won't set foot in my car, and she sure won't let me into the bedroom.

Molly scrubs.

Her sister applies the wet feed sack strip to the window crack, the one side where the dust blows in worst.

A corner of land blown right off, he says. I just wanted to stomp the land back down. Weeds grow anyway, why not what I try to plant?

Molly starts sobbing.

He looks at her sister, they both step away from Molly's shaking shoulders as if the kitchen were huge, they step back.

Four months almost to the day, he says, and shivers. She was watching him just fine in that room. I don't see why she thinks she wasn't.

Stray dust smacks the window.

Even wrapped him with rags of turpentine, says her sister. He hardly even coughed.

Molly coughs, gets up off her knees and, stumbling, runs back into the bedroom again.

Her sister starts pressing the strip into the window wood but the top of the strip is so heavy with paste it bows and peels down. You could help, she says.

He stands at the threshold of the bedroom, then he doesn't, he is over by the stove, he is beside her. He holds the strip into place while she rubs more paste onto another, more flour they don't have much of, less water.

His arm sweats not so far from hers, his filthy hand is right next to her face.

The sister bites his thumb.

He doesn't pull it away. She bites him again, holding the new strip against the dust that is coming no matter what she does.

BOMB JOCKEY

The stub of a town kicks up its legs, puts on an actual parade for those who'll decide which town gets the bomb works, her daddy being one of the deciders, a tall heavy-nosed state politician who looks good in a suit when others don't. His wife comes along for the parade, and their daughter hands out flyers coincident with the next election.

Hump takes two.

The other guys keep their hands in their pockets once they *Thank you ma'am* her. Hump doesn't even look at the flyer before he wants another. Known as Hump to his face, a face that looks enough like John Wayne's that some people think he ought to get a rope and start in with a lariat, if not a horse, he is not as shy as he could be since you don't get to be eighteen looking like that without some serious experience. Nearby a Marybeth is trying to wound him grievously by flirting with a boy from the next town, a Colette slinks around in a long dress in this ninety-five-degree parade weather in the middle of a float that reads: *We're ready if you are,* and a Nancy wears nothing under her band jacket just in case.

He pockets those flyers without looking at them because he is looking at the politician's daughter.

35

Vote Walker, she yells. He'll give you what you want. Vote Walker, you won't regret it. She stands dark-eyed, dark-haired, red-lipped, and tall.

Chewing gum? he asks when she takes a breath. He holds a stick up to her face, hoping to quiet her.

Kind of you, she says, taking it and unwrapping it. She pops it into her mouth and shouts, Vote Walker.

I thought you might be getting hoarse. He sidles himself a little closer. He is wide through the chest and thin at the waist, he can get close.

She chews, she nods. He extracts his flyers from his pocket and waves them beside her, shouting, Vote Walker.

At the end of the parade that turns out short, due to the size of the town and not its enthusiasm, her father struts over the way a politician will, handshaking Hump with his right hand and working the boy's shoulder muscle with his left. We'll get the bomb works built here in no time, son. Don't you worry about that. As long as the vote goes my way.

I think you have a chance, says Hump. At least here. We don't get many running for the big offices that come around here.

Oh, I'm partial to seeing to the will of the people on this issue, says the politician, his hand moving to the back of his daughter's neck as if he is about to herd her from Hump. He goes on despite constituents beelining toward him: Not just the capital's. When people anywhere talk, I give a listen. With the war on, a bomb plant is just what you need out here. Why, you could be a bomb jockey.

The politician pretends a gallop.

The one-armed photographer from the paper takes a picture of the three of them. Just imagine this whole place lit up with new enterprise, the photographer says, his buggy, black beanhole eyes as lit up as his camera flash.

I'll do my best, says the politician as if he will, looking around for his wife who is caught up in a swirl of voters. Say, he says to this cowboy standing too close to his daughter, why aren't you signed up to fight?

Sole support, he says. A crippled mother. He gives the girl a sidelong look.

She is watching the parade-watchers fold their chairs.

I'm sorry to hear that, says the politician, with a nod of suspicion. This kid with his handsomeness, with his thumbs hooked to his belt loops and enough of a grin to signal he can take whatever he gets, nods back.

Help my girl pack the rest of the flyers out to my car, why don't you? says the politician. He gestures toward the bale of flyers behind her. Show him where, he says to his daughter.

Hump hauls the bale.

He isn't giving her the *Where to?* look most men he imagines give her in the pretty big town she comes from. He is taking his time so she can inspect him, a specimen she could not have had much recent experience with: nearly all the able-bodied have flocked to the draft. He looks very able-bodied. She leads him through the waist-high weeds into the lot her mother parked the car beside. Are you a religious nut? she asks. Is that really why you haven't been drafted?

You have no manners, he says, and then raises the bale of flyers with one finger over her head as if she should now take them from him.

My ankle, she screeches, turning her heel on a weed. Ouch! she says and drops herself suddenly but not too violently to the ground. That hurt, she mews.

Miss Walker, he says. Miss? He drops the bundle of flyers to the ground and bends over to check the damage.

She catches him by the neck and pulls him to her so far down that the weeds hide them both. Now I am both a girl of virtue and my father's daughter but here—she kisses him on the cheek—you can kiss me back.

I can do better than that, he says, and puckers up right on her mouth and passes his gum to her.

She spits it out. You idiot.

Pretty low, he says, falling like that. He walks off without the flyers.

✳

Munroe is Bomb County says the crepe paper stuffed into the chicken wire county map bumping to the end of the short front street that he crosses in a hurry, followed by *Progress and Jobs* pricked into a play bomb with red hearts and encircled by papier-mâché shrapnel strung on hangers. No one would guess they were hangers unless you are one of the girls exiting the next float who follows his progress. They wear satin sashes printed with *Munroe County Votes for the Army* and stick out their busts so there can be no mistake in the reading. Just behind them mill the band members, the younger boys in town and a few old winos. They have just finished blowing and beating the bigger instruments, the tuba, bass drum, and trombone, trying to look employable and hardworking to the ordnance people.

All of them set to entertaining themselves and the brass with a pie-eating contest (*a state official wins!*), a barbecue (*free drinks for the judges!*), a Parade of Prize Pets (*get Mamie's pig out of here!*), some singing and dancing from a vaudeville act of two hoofers that are sent for special from the capital—no one skips any of it, least of all Hump and the politician's daughter, the two of them never quite out of sight of each other, squaring off finally only after it gets dark, when he offers to take her to the cliff where Indians ran whole herds of buffalo over, even horses, a cliff that everybody in the entire state wants to see, even in the moonlight, or so he says.

Though still sore about his gum trick, she has to admit a touch of curiosity. Does this local really think he can make time with her? Her parents are out enjoying a grand fund-raising party and she's already seen the movie in town, sitting in her own town's grand theater—she has no real excuse to turn tail.

Walking the short way to the edge of town, they discuss the movie's gangster and his moll, their clever getaway. I saw it twice. She could really drive, he says. Can you drive like that?

As often as I can, she says. But with gas rations, and my father—he wants me to live long enough to collect a crown in this year's pageant.

The state contest? he says. That will soon enough be over.

She plucks at what looks like a wild black-eyed Susan in the dark. You mean I won't win?

He rises to her perturbation. You'll take the trophy and leave for an even bigger place than the capital, he says. Yankton.

She laughs. I've been to bigger. She twirls her flower by the stem. You want to see my talent? I can spin plates, she says.

A dishwasher can do that, he says.

She gives him a smile that even in the moonlit night glows lipstick-red. My sister's competing too.

You have a lot of sisters? He walks closer.

One brother and four sisters. My eldest sister has been engaged three times. We are not optimistic.

And yourself?

She stands at the cliff, looking over. I can't be in the pageant if I'm engaged, she says. It's a rule.

He leads her to a dip in the cliff, where nobody can spot them. With the moon all the way up and not much more talk, they swing their legs over the edge and try a few other ways of kissing—without gum—until it is time to find her family car.

Hump drinks a sip of coffee from his canteen and screws up his face at its cold bitterness. His buddies are probing their shovels into the tough prairie grass to find the easiest spot to bury the turkeys, the dead or at least dead-ish bombs. Shingles stick up nearby, tapped into place to show where they buried previous turkeys, with fast-fading location numbers painted across them, some of the shingles already fallen over and blown a few feet off.

I hate the burying, says Hump, walking over with his own shovel. It's so morbid.

Yeah, well, says Matthews, a conscientious objector who wears a full beard "like Jesus" so nobody gets confused about what he's here for.

The short guy Fred is on his toes, studying a rained-on piece of graph paper spread on the big truck's hood. He's a little more in charge than the others, being that he presses his shirts by laying them flat under his mattress, and doesn't chase girls all the time. I think we got leeway here, he says. Is that a five or a two that shows where they want them?

Why don't you check the carbon of the orders? says Matthews.

Somebody smart left it on the dash and now it's all faded. Fred holds a second paper up to the sun.

Matthews leans into his shovel. The wind gets up in their hesitation.

So why don't we just drive on over to that new blowout and put them in where the soil is looser? says Hump.

If you'd been listening to the lieutenant, you'd know why, says Fred. Anyway, we don't get to decide much. You are always thinking, he says to Hump, about how to do it easier.

Hump doesn't deny his thoughtfulness. The other two are the problem: Otto's half Sioux but he works like a German and people think he's a spy. Really, when he hears *Shovel,* despite his pigeon-toed shoveling, he has to hear *Stop* before he lays it down, which is why they put him with Matthews, who is less than thrilled about the work, as angry as he is about war. It doesn't make it any easier that the two of them share a tent on government property. But Matthews is already changing his digging style, spading in a nice long trench for one bomb and then the other, and not the coffin-looking pit they usually dig, not so shallow.

They can't fire us, says Matthews. There's nobody else to do the work.

Put them close together, Fred says, not even thinking anymore about *no.*

Slave driver. You ought to write the manual, says Hump, moving Otto into place.

I sure would put a few more things into it, Fred says, starting to work his shovel in the trench alongside Matthews.

Otto points to looming thunderheads. They get to digging faster. The sun is hanging way past lunch position when they finish. No one suggests they stop and eat what they've brought along, they are hopped up fully, they are nervous and smiley. Fred backs the truck up to the long hole and they crank down the first sling until the shell is all nestled in, then they slide the sling out from under it ever so gently.

The shell drools at its seams. Maybe it is new drool, it is hard to tell because the corrosion sets in so fast once it gets started. You'd think the war would be over by now, with so many bombs they get screwed-up, but no, quality control is just catching up. The men are even slower getting the second one out of the truck as it looks even worse. They sacrifice its sling it looks so bad, leaving the sling looped under its belly right where they lay it, then they are supposed to pack in the dirt as if it is cotton balls. Fred starts dusting it with light loads.

Duds for the duds is what that lieutenant called us. Hump is angry. Just because we're not enlisted. His shovelful smacks the shell.

Ding! A loose rock from Otto hits hard. Something starts to tick.

All of them drop their tools, run behind the truck, and plug their ears with their fingers.

The wind blows and a tumbleweed tumbles.

What do you call a chicken that crosses the road for a girl? asks Hump.

Hump, says Fred, making a girly swivel.

They all whistle, then Hump lobs two more big clods of dirt at the shell.

Ding!

Dirt twists up where one clod misses.

This is the real dud, yells Hump, and he hefts a clod twice as big as the others, jumps out from behind the truck and does a jitterbug and a turn with it. Like it? he shouts. He throws the clod straight at the bomb, and dives behind the truck again.

Nothing.

Otto answers Hump by doing something similar, although stumbly, his pigeon-toes crossing. Then Fred runs out. Fred sure isn't stopping them, not by a long shot.

You are all chickenshit, shouts Matthews, hunting around for a piece that is bigger than all of theirs, the biggest. The earth isn't as rocky there so he has to search through what they've dug up to find something. He comes across a clump with a big bone sticking out of it, no time to see what kind of animal. Peace, he yells as he throws it. He nearly falls over, he is trying so hard to outdo them.

The two bombs burst at once and rain earth as if the earth is coming apart at the seams. They all inhale it, each of them raccoon-eyed with a mud mask after. Matthew is thrown a ways away.

What a mother, says Hump, gasping for breath, the filth running off him. Who would have thought it could be wet enough for mud down there? I'll be.

A curl of blood from Otto's nose is making its way down the mud near his mouth. He shakes his head and his braid waves. He wipes his nose on the back of his hand and sits up. That was fun, he coughs.

Fred and Hump beat each other on the back. Matthews shakes his head in disapproval while a big guilty smile is breaking across his face. His glasses are broken.

A grass fire has caught over by the truck and they put it out with the loose dirt they shovel from the hole. By the time they are loaded up again, it is about four, and the land has a seeped-in pond with shrapnel for rocks, the bomb-scorched area is covered with fresh earth, and some unplanned rock spew has cracked the truck's windshield.

We'll say the truck could've blown, says Fred in a voice higher than usual, inspecting the wrecked windshield. The turkeys were that bad.

It could happen just like that, says Hump, snapping his fingers.

Nobody wants to ride in back, they are still too jittery and scared. They all squeeze into the cab and Fred roars off as if he doesn't want to stick around another second.

Over there—see that antelope? Otto leans forward on the dash, bleeding again, using his left-hand fingers to pinch his nose closed, the others to point.

You are a damned Indian with deer, says Matthews. You can't be smelling them.

Otto smiles happy. A herd of antelope that have to be at least ten miles away they are that small skip-run across the plains.

Fred turns his mud-masked face to Hump. Hot damn, he says. We're all just crazy.

They whoop, whoop so loud the herd disappears.

Hump's great-aunt fusses and prepares food that he ignores while he borrows her phone to call the pageant. It is the last day and he has sat up on the munitions train all night to get to the capital in time. The receiver at the pageant end gets passed around, girl by girl, until she claims it. Come to the party after the ceremony, she says. She gives him an address that his great-aunt scrutinizes and then advises him to bathe, and bathe well. Good luck, she says, scraping his plate. I will sponge your jacket.

He hasn't thought about luck. He's always had it with girls. But this one certainly didn't sound at all surprised by his call. Probably guys are always driving clear across the state to sit at her feet. He pulls an actual comb through his hair and ponders the position of his part. He's brought clothes he hasn't much considered, other than his arms and legs go through the holes. He has chosen them to fit though, and his great-aunt shakes her head when he emerges from the bathroom. You'll give somebody a run for her money, she says, and he is not the least embarrassed.

Don't wait up, he says.

Me? I'm going to bed early on account of the shock of your arrival, she says, patting him on the head as if it were six years ago, and him just an ornery boy on his first and only prior visit.

He walks across town toward one of the built-up neighborhoods, double-time, arms windmilling, legs charging, then slows at a cross street to the sound of the roar of a crowd through open windows.

The party is swank, a Judge someone under the doorbell, maybe a friend of her father's but no doubt a judge of beauty too, given the nice size of the house and the good paint job. He finds what must be a sibling lolling about in a party clump, a girl who looks about right but isn't her. He can't ask her where his girl is, he is supposed to know—anyway, he is supposed to pretend to know. He takes a sandwich from a tray and wanders the dance floor, dodging jitterbuggers throwing girls around, so many he wonders if there are more girls now than at peacetime. There are certainly more soldiers than ever, drab groups eyeing the girls in swarms. He dodges them too, thankful he isn't in a white shirt to be mistaken for a drink-handler, and locates a harp player in the living room and a three-piece ensemble on the lawn, but not her. Her he spots sitting on a piece of wicker on a porch facing the lawn, eating grapes. A guy in uniform is peeling one of the grapes with his teeth. No. He walks a little closer and sees the guy is just swallowing the grapes one at a time, then he is saying, See you, doll, whenever you get patriotic.

Uniforms bore me, she says to the soldier's back. They are so—uniform, she says as the soldier drifts off, then she sees him standing in front of her.

Sweetheart, he says, and then six or seven words in a row.

He drops his sandwich beside the grapes on a plate. They jitterbug all over the lawn to the band that blasts out the window, they push off from each others' palms and twirl under arms and even legs until the music rags the air right out of them. She falls into his arms for a slow dance and he glides her toward a set of stairs that other pageant contestants still parade up and down, drinks in hand and smoking—both vices exactly what they swore in pageantry promotion to abhor. Upstairs, he finds a study with a grandfather clock and a closed door and he twirls her forward.

The radio mentioned your name, he says. I had to come.

Liar, she says. The radio didn't say a thing about me.

He pulls her close and kisses her. When he starts in with *Too bad about,* she puts her fingers to his lips and acts out the highlights: how she went plate-crazy with half a kitchen suspended on sticks—her breasts shiver while her hands circle in demonstration—and then, she says, a plate ricocheted off to the floor. She stuck her arm out quick to collect it like she meant to and then she bowed with the other three plates tucked, and gave a big smile to the next contestant.

He claps, relaxing back in the chair.

While I was changing into my bathing suit the next county's queen said: You used strings on those plates, right? Calm as anything, I said: Then how could I lose one? But the judges didn't see it as a stunt either, they marked me with a penalty for dropping a plate and went for the snake charmer, a girl with a drugged python around her neck but a wriggling way with the flute and sequins. She couldn't have lost.

He sees her point, which she makes snake-like.

Still, she aced Bathing Suits. He imagines her sashaying past Miss Citizens National Bank and those two girls who, she says, weren't even really old enough to compete, he sees her swivel the way she does for him on the rug, hands to hips, all that long leg now hidden under her skirt. Before he can really grasp that situation, that is to say, run his hand over that hip, saying, I wish I could have seen it all, she says: It's annoying to have a beau ogling the other beauties at work. Clever of you to show up now.

Yes, ma'am, he says, all innocence.

Three partygoers wander in and offer them olives which they found "all alone" in the judge's pantry. They are strictly rationed, they say, giving each of them only one.

He swallows the pit—what else can he do?—while she talks on, holding her own aloft and intact.

I wore a red, white, and blue outfit with the stars across my front and stripes on the skirt and held myself like this— she lifts her chin—and, she says, the whole while I told them about pacifism so clearly it was as if I made it up myself. *As a woman I can't go to war, and I refuse to send anyone else.* I used Jeanette Rankin's very words. She was the first woman elected to Congress. From Montana, no less. They applauded, she says, as if they were thinking with their hands. She claps slowly, to show him. Selling war bonds is the reason for the whole shebang, the contest and everything. Why, the banks are in on the war too.

If I remember right, he says, Rankin had to hide in a phone booth after she was the only person to vote against the war. She hid there until the police could get her home.

Competing in a pageant is the closest thing to real politics a woman can get most of the time. I had to keep my speech a secret, even from the likes of you. Two of my sisters went all the way to Atlantic City.

She gives him her olive. He swallows the pit again while she watches, amused. Gorgeous, she says, that's dangerous.

You have to come out and see a few of the big shells go off, he says. My friend Matthews is a CO. We call him our commanding officer.

That's funny, she says, moving a little closer.

You were definitely the most beautiful.

The grandfather clock strikes some late hour while they kiss. Her will, her rebelliousness excites him. He is contrary himself, not running off to the front lines, mother or no mother, like plenty of other guys. He loves to sucker punch the cowboys in the bar back home about it. I actually deal with bombs, he told them. I'm not standing there waiting for the bombs to hit me, I'm actually putting my arms around them.

He has his arms tight around her, his Miss Dakota, Miss Galaxy, Miss Universe, His Miss.

They finish kissing about five minutes after somebody flashes the lights to try to get rid of them. Spurning the joyriders, those people piling into a Studebaker with the gas ration prize, he walks her home all the way across town. Arm-in-arm, and with him about to jitterbug her forward for a last kiss he has quite fully imagined, they are met by her father at the door, who must've heard them laughing.

Margaret, says her father. His tone says *No fooling.* He takes her by the elbow and tows her inside.

She waves her loose arm.

You didn't think, did you? her father roars. Still dressed in the suit he wore to the pageant, he is not exactly sober and walks that way, teetering forward on his shoe tips.

She takes a seat beside her robe-clad mother, who points to the side table where the morning newspaper screams *Pageant Pacifist.* Everything I said was true, says the girl.

I'm trying to get elected, he says. The votes will be close, very close.

She purses her lips but she knows this is also true.

He drinks, he puts down his glass. While I wish it were different, that is the reality of the situation. How long is it before college starts?

Three months, her mother says. More or less.

Well, you can't wait around here. You'll remind people.

He finds her a government job collecting TB results for some hospital reckoning. Her sister should chaperone her as she travels, train by train, through the state, but instead she comes down with a cough because a certain someone of hers has leave in the capital, at least that first month. But the schedule for her collecting certainly isn't passed around for her sister's or her parents' inspection, especially since it makes plain her first stop.

All day she sits in the little town's infirmary, having assembled most of the right files in about ten minutes. For the rest, she'll have to return in a week. Maybe a couple of returns, it is that chaotic around here, what with the shortage of help, she writes in her report. The train ride back won't happen again for hours. She hears from the nurses that the workers are pouring cement for structures called igloos—setting a record, says one of them, thirty-two in a single shift.

Igloos?

You can walk up the side of an igloo, says the nurse. They cover a Quonset with cement and then grass, like it grew out of the ground. The engineers figure that dirt will put a damper on any explosion. Not that there will be any explosions. It's a surprise that any of these shells ever go off in enemy territory is what they always say, says the nurse, sorting instruments. Igloos, she says, shaking her head. Keeps the bombs cool.

She laughs the way she is supposed to. She doesn't think about danger, she thinks about him setting a record. Sitting in that clinic playing tic-tac-toe on the pad in front of her, she spots a cement truck making regular trips past the office, with an arm hanging out the window she might know. During a walk she happens to take for air just then, she waves, and he downshifts like a demon, sending himself practically through the windshield.

You could hurt a fellow waving that hand of yours around, he says out his window.

I was just fixing my hair, she says.

Oh, god, he says, like he wants to touch it.

Aren't you going to ask me to lunch? It's lunchtime.

She lets him park and together they walk toward the café filling up with ranchers and other good gossipers. You can come to the rodeo with me tonight, he says. I'll bet you've never been to one of those.

What makes you think I'll have the time? she says.

You'll change your ticket.

Maybe. She leans toward him and sniffs. That's not cement.

Perfume of the devil, TNT. He puffs his chest forward. About the most powerful explosive in the world.

She inhales big. I just love it.

My mother sells these dolls at the rodeo that she makes out of cornstalks. The Indians showed her how, since we live so close to where Custer made his stand. Although she's about as Irish as they come, he says. Ma will say in the Irish way, I don't remember a lass like you in his class in high school.

You're nervous, she laughs.

I've tried all the other feelings out on you. Listen, she's making lemonade.

From the next room, she can hear ice flung into a pitcher.

I have to change, he says.

She fidgets with the doily his mother has put out to hide the crack in the top of the side table. Out the window of a small front room pink peonies border the chain link that she hardly has time to admire before his mother rolls in on her wheelchair.

I'm not in his class, she says to his mother before she can ask. We met the day of the bomb parade.

His mother is grand in design the way somebody confined to a chair gets to be, but with good looks in decline, and nicely salt-and-pepper wire-haired. Class? she says. He ought not to be thinking about class. Blarney—he should be thinking about money.

He is fast-buttoning a rodeo shirt in his bedroom, about as defenseless as a man can be.

She takes a breath. What are your thoughts about the war?

His mother is sorting through the basket of cornstalks at her feet. He's got the best job for the war. It's safe here and he still gets to blow things up. He once stuck a firecracker in the middle of his birthday cake. After it went off, we had icing to the rafters.

It is hot in here, he says, coming through the door. I've got to get you a fan.

You've got to get tickets to the rodeo for yourself and your date and push my ten-ton chair closer to the window so I can hear the loudspeakers, that's all in god's name what you've got to do. His mother jabs a needle at a bug that has escaped a cornstalk.

An announcer's voice already blares beyond the open window, and a crowd roars back in laughter.

I have the tickets, he says as he maneuvers her chair in place. The lieutenant gave them out yesterday.

The virtues of employment, says his mother. There will be barrel racing tonight, and people on horses doing the figure eights with maypoles. The Army Depot thinks it's good for morale, all the civilians working while everybody else's morale gets kept up by killing the Germans. They're even providing all the free pints you can drink. You'd better believe the morale will be high.

The girl nods at all that straight talk. I'm a pacifist, she says.

I guess that means you won't fight with me, says his mother.

Her boy squats down fast in front of her chair, in an almost eye-to-eye position. Wish me luck, Mom. I'm going to get in there with them, I'm going to volunteer and win the watch.

The bull, he means he's going to get in there with the bull and pull off the watch off its horn, says his mother, patting him on the ear. You idiot. What a way to volunteer! And in front of the likes of her.

The girl stares at the rough cornstalk doll in her hand, just about twisted to a finish. I'm grown, she says. And so is he.

That's not what I meant. His mother lifts her thick black brows. He handles that truck pretty well but he doesn't know much about animals. He didn't even keep a dog when he was little. What makes you think you can charm a watch off a raging bull? Half the town's girls maybe.

Let's go, he says to her. Before she tells you the whole truth.

Fewer locals than last year push their way down through the crowded bleachers toward the bull because those who aren't at the bomb site are fighting or dead from fighting or else not right in the head from fighting and are locked away. The free beer spills as they push through the crowd, fueling a ripe smell in the late-afternoon-to-evening stench of barnyard and heat. There's been roping and bull riding and barrel racing and now's the time for the crowd to get in on the act. Only the bull with its hoofs locked in a stance, with its head down, which reads tired to some—the dumb ones—has the sense to stay in the deepening shade.

Fred and Hump squeeze up against the gate, on the lookout for Otto. Matthews is sick from a hot dog but Fred tells Hump he's been like that all day, nauseous ever since they unpacked the leaking mustard shells. All week they've laid bets on whether Otto will even come to the rodeo. Although his braids keep him from being called a Kraut, here he has to face a lot of cowboys. When he does finally show, he waves at Hump's girl left behind high in the bleachers, and she waves back.

A recorded trumpet blares and the announcer goes on about the bull, trying one off-color remark after another, ending each time with an *Excuse me, ladies.* Hump looks up at his girl again, fanning herself with the program. He senses impatience, her worry about catching the last train.

No, he says to Otto when he tries to give Hump the rest of his beer. I need to see straight.

The gate splits open and all the men run at the bull, the watch flashing on its horn. Lots of them work in pairs, one waving his hands, the other rushing him. Overall, the effect confounds the animal that rears back on its legs the better to charge them with and then does, coming so close to goring a slow fellow that his bandana flies off in the rush. The crowd lets out wild shrieks because in a second, all the men go in again, with a clump of them thinking to surprise it, Hump and Fred loud among them. Otto can't help himself. His feet, being a bit turned in, trip him, and after his recovery, two or three others block his escape.

Get 'em, boys, says the announcer, as quick as the bull snorts. Hump skitters a little to the right and touches its horn, feels it real. That is enough for him. He hops away.

The bull lowers his head and makes a quick shift the way such a big animal can, and catches Otto stumbling and flips him. He lands sitting up, legs spread wrong, his eyes blinking as if the light of day is now altogether too bright. About a foot off sits the watch, somehow slipped from the horn. Otto leans way forward but can't quite reach it. He is hurt.

The bull sits down too.

While an ambulance with its emergency wail makes its way into the arena and the high school band plays *Like It or Not* in a jazzy way, Hump glimpses the lieutenant's moment of glee— he is doubled over, laughing—and he quick kicks the watch to Otto through the dust.

The announcer screams: We have a winner! when Otto holds the watch up. The crowd roars. The gate opens up again so real clowns can convince the bull to leave the ring, herd it away from all the disappointed drunks who are climbing the fence they are in such a hurry to get out.

Otto tosses the watch back at Hump. You take it—she'll like it, he shouts. It's got a radium dial.

Then he faints dead away.

This is a bad idea, she says, this closet. The nurses' break is almost over.

It wasn't bad the last three times. He is mouthing the words.

She isn't taking off her bra. She lets him feel around it, touch beneath it, she lets him whisk around deep in the cleavage with his tongue but no, that is it. Look at the biceps on you, she whispers, and touches his left arm's set, not what he is pressing against her.

He says, Let's, you know—what's the matter?

Someone's feet block the light under the closet door, a shuffle, then a start. They let their breaths out. She rises on her elbows and he is back to a squat. I am going back to college, she whispers. I have bought the clothes.

You go for Matthews, don't you? he says roughly. All his no-war talk.

She pushes him away. She feels tears, a very unfamiliar surge of them, coming on. There they are, as womanly as you get. She backhands them. Pretty boy, she whispers. It's not that.

Someone blocks the light again at the door, probably wanting clean towels, she says, folding the new shirt of his he's laid on the floor.

Okay. He rearranges himself, fingers back his hair. But it is lunchtime, nobody is ever around now, he reminds her, leaning toward her for another kiss.

The feet won't go away. Someone clears his throat.

Okay, I'll stay, he says. You go.

She repins her hair, she tries not to kiss him again but his face is so close to hers and he has his arms around her. The kiss goes on and on.

The feet—*tap tap tap*—leave.

Good thing, she says at last, with a gasp. She opens the door and takes two steps into the rest room across the hall, combs, lipsticks.

A nurse is loading the closet on her way out. Where's he gone? He isn't supposed to use the window across the hall but there it is, not quite closed. She closes it. She sees him outside, catty-corner, talking to another nurse, probably the one who stood in front of the door, but it doesn't look as if he is in trouble, it looks as if he is making trouble, smiling and touching the brim of his hat.

She cries then into the privacy of a handkerchief. Then the front door rings and someone walks in, saying Margaret? Margaret?

She wipes her eyes. It's the nurse, smiling. He said if I saw you in here to give you this. She hands her a small flat box. It looks like it might be hose, she says, winking. But there's something rolling around inside.

Thank you, she says, and puts on her best smile and just keeps on smiling until the nurse goes to look for a clipboard. She doesn't tip the box to hear whatever rattles in there with the hose because that would be telling, and she won't.

It is her last day of a whole summer's worth of stalling over the TB numbers and it is her last day, period. She sees his truck bed as it turns off the street. She blows her nose. She refuses the shotgun solution—she won't give herself to him that way.

It isn't—how does her father put it?—unilateral. Besides, she isn't that pregnant.

By the time Hump daydreams the truck back to work, Fred has almost polished the pits off a big shell's chrome. I thought it was okay to be gassing them, Fred is saying to Matthews, who is helping him move the shell next to the rabbit cage.

There's been conventions against it for years, says Matthews. He shrugs. It's what the Brits did in Iraq in the twenties. He turns and collects a wrench.

I like knowing secrets, says Otto. He drags his rodeo cast across the inside of the shed, chrome tailings collecting around his toes.

Secrets like why do we have to carry rabbits with us now? asks Hump, settling his foot on an apple box, not ready to work yet.

I am not frightened by rabbits, says Matthews.

I'll be damned if I have to chase them, says Otto.

Fred wiggles his fingers for rabbit ears.

I'll bet you only get about another ten minutes to live, given the difference in size between rabbits and us, says Matthews.

Look into a dung heap and you see worms, Hump says. We're already up to here in it. He glances out the window at the clear blue sky.

Otto nods and nods, as if the motion will bring on disagreement, but Hump is in suspense about his girl and not in the least argumentative, and wears that new shirt to prove it.

You look like a courting man, says Fred after he finishes all his polishing.

Other clothes wore out, says Hump.

I can believe it, says Matthews, wrestling a gas canister to his workbench. Off and on, on and off.

She's got a powerful arm on her from all that plate-spinning, says Fred.

Arm? says Matthews.

Arm? says Otto.

Hump cuffs Otto, who can't stop laughing. The subject of Hump's girl is closed.

She is sitting on the steps of the courthouse, his box in her hand, with the two cartons of files from the clinic next to her. He puts his head out the truck window, his hair sticking straight up with hair tonic or fear of her—a fuse. She can't help but kiss him at least on the cheek, and he returns the kiss big. He stows the clinic cartons in the back, then moves his rabbit cage to one side so there is more room for her.

Call her Rosie. Rosie the Riveter, she tells him. She sings a few lines from the truck radio: *Keeps a sharp lookout for sabotage, / Sitting up there on the fuselage. / That little girl will do more than a male will do.* She sighs after the song is over and holds out his box to him. I'm giving this back.

My mother took the ring off years ago after my father left. Keep it, he says, hardly steering. You're going to need it later, if not right away. I don't want to have to get up my courage again.

Courage? You sweet-talked that nurse into giving it to me. She laughs at his assurance, his persistence. College, she says, touching the rabbit through the screen. No ring.

He gives her the smallest kiss her cheek has ever felt, although her whole self is not an inch away. Rosie? he says for want of anything else to say after she climbs out of the truck.

That's her name, she says, nodding despite her rejection. But his brisk *See you* at the train car as he hands her the forgotten files manages to make her so angry she boards it in a righteous huff.

He tries to call her but the dorm doesn't take messages or if they do, she doesn't return them.

If she wants to be like that.

The way he sets to at the gun club range, six targets untouched, not even the rim, the sergeant won't let him back in for a month.

She miscarries on a date with some childhood friend. She is drunk and dancing beside a bonfire in the sand next to a lake dug out for a big dam, one of her father's deeds and works that same election year, dancing and dancing and dancing even though she knows it is all bunk about shaking it loose, she dances anyway until she gets lucky. She is bent double when she sends her date off to find her purse in the car parked about a half mile away, and she buries what is still just a blood clot in the hauled-in sand. The next morning she picks up the phone to say *Hump* into the receiver but she doesn't dial. Not a month after that she tries out an engagement with a quiet sophomore with thick glasses. I could be the enemy and drop a bomb and you wouldn't even notice, she yells at him the night she rips his ring off her finger. At least she still has that watch from the rodeo. But is that from Otto or Hump? In her limbo of confusion, she earns straight A's in English.

Maybe Hump hops the train to the capital to moon around her neighborhood and maybe he doesn't, maybe he is so busy mooning around other high-class girls who live around there he doesn't have the time to waste.

Meanwhile, Otto cracks off his cast—it went all the way to his waist—and now he can dance. His new feet don't turn in anymore, not one whit.

Autumn falls on all of them, its tumbleweeds, its wetter weather, its dark, then winter arrives anyway. She volunteers to drive five college seniors back home for Christmas in someone's old jalopy, and not so far from his town, she leaves the car in the wrong gear so long it starts to smoke. She does not stop but the car stops for her, another ten miles further. A smile crosses her face when she announces the news, puzzling the groaning girls who are laden with finery *in extremis*: boxes, suitcases roped shut, even a cage with a bird one girl couldn't possibly leave behind. After a flagged-down farmer loads all this into the back of his truck, he asks which town she would like to try her luck in about the matter of a garage, and of course she picks the one she knows.

The waitress at the café remembers her well enough to have a conversation but she's short, more interested in the mercury spill she saw on her way to work. How beautiful and strange the great gobs of liquid metal were, slithering all over the ground in amongst the snowed-in crocuses. Mrs. Olmstead's fifth-grade class has already paid a visit to play with it. Another advantage of having the army store their bullets and what-all here. Like a science fair day in and day out, she says.

Like most people, the only mercury the girls have ever seen wandered inside a glass thermometer until somebody dropped it. Gallons of mercury! Imagine—a riverful by the end of it, according to a local who hooks his hat just inside the door a few minutes later. Glistening silver like you'd want it on your wedding wish list.

What happened to it all? someone asks the waitress, who doesn't know, who just repeats the question to the local, who says it sinks into the ground after a while, there's no catching it. It's quicksilver, you know? Although he's scooped up a little, do they all want to have a look?

The girls and the waitress and the cashier crowd around him. He slides a quart whisky bottle out of his coat that is stoppered with newspaper and he pours the contents into his soup bowl, empty except for a few cigarette ashes and now this quivering silver.

This is nothing, he says to their admiration. I've got some rocks the Indians give me last year. They glow all night, he says and smiles at all the ladies, as if in invitation to stay up and watch the glow with him. Like that dial there, he says, pointing at the watch around her wrist.

The busboy collects the man's water glass, his spoon and paper napkin. Take it all, the man says, adding the empty whisky bottle to the soup bowl with the mercury. It's just trash anyway. There's nothing you can do with it, he says to the women. Like money in your pocketbooks.

That barrel was probably too small for what they put in it, says the man in greasy mechanic's clothes who has come in at last. Always trying too hard to increase their productivity. Change the oil now and then in that car of yours, along with the gears, he says to her, tipping his hat. It makes a hell of a difference. It'll take me until tomorrow to do the repair.

The girls smoke the afternoon away, then pool their money and rent a single room at the Corner Hotel. There they curl their hair and laugh about who will get whom out of the rough lot in the café. They paint their nails.

College girls! By nightfall, all seven hundred workers know they've arrived. An invasion, says Fred, dropping a tool in the rehab shed. Matthews says Fred's too skittish to be trusted with munitions, let alone a woman. Otto twirls a wrench. So many men make the trip to town stuffed into cars and trucks suddenly needing supplies, skipping their ballgame and their dinners, that there is a traffic jam on the main street, guys hanging out of jalopies, whistling so loud all the dogs in town come running.

They tour the government's new sketched-out town, Hump turning a flashlight here and there so she can see how much is happening: side streets and hospitals, little red-flagged stakes sticking out of the snow to show where the lots end and the prairie starts. You can't say it's not the right name for it, she says, when he tells her they are going to call it Igloo. We'll have built eight hundred of them in six months for the facility. He tries to stay mostly informative. Where's his anger after all those months of not seeing her? He's giddy.

He tells her all about the real igloos and about how noisy the Arctic is, how he's heard penguins raise quite a ruckus and stink, and that the Eskimos keep to their igloos for more reasons than just to keep warm. He tries twice to get his cold hands inside her coat. He knows it was an old ploy, the oldest, probably people used it in the Ice Age, not just the Eskimos is what he tells her. She bats his hands away, and he tucks them, not really so frozen, under his armpits. I'm thinking of joining the Foreign Legion where it's nice and warm.

The desert is cold at night. She's not looking at him.

A lot of belly dancers there.

If that's what you want. She starts walking ahead of him.

The little starter town falls behind them until even the road-grader ruts run out. They are soon walking on blown-clean prairie, stars burning at the black if they wanted to look at them, but he's head-down, behind her, kicking at a dirt clod. He has to raise his voice. It's not fair that they won't let a guy have a house in Igloo unless he's married. Like it's not a real job until then. Even Fred is thinking about girls.

It's a real job, she says, her heels sinking into the soft spots so she lets him catch her arm. There are just no medals involved.

Lots of medals in the desert.

But they're in French. She says she heard that people weren't supposed to drink the water around here. It's bad, she says.

The plumbing's fine, he sputters. We're putting in our own water system. You just think we're all savages, drinking river runoff full of rabbit pellets.

No, she says, that's not what I think.

Look at that. A valentine.

From where they stand, runoff has made a heart-shaped puddle, and when a cloud moves off the moon, the liquid is pink and chemical crystals dot the edges.

She lets him kiss her, then one of his hands slide inside her coat, and she lets that corpse-cold hand in even under her sweater until it comes to life. You some kind of spy with a hand like that? she asks.

They see nothing of the second feature. Horses gallop, shots are fired, men suffer hanging, and women weep, but they take no notice. Popcorn from the other college girls alights and bounces off them. Fred and Matthews and then Otto hoot. Everybody but the two of them exits at the end for the church basement where there is said to be a record player. It isn't as if the elderly usher hasn't seen couples like them before. He sweeps out the popcorn from the rows in front and behind with his long-handled broom, then pokes Hump on the shoulder with the tip end. Nice night? he asks.

Nice, she says softly while Hump glares.

There's mercury on his shirt that catches the light in the foyer.

Hump likes to take a secret smoke about five miles away from the depot before the next army train shows. They all like a break. Hump unpockets his cigarettes and matches, hunches in the cab with Fred and Matthews. Otto's outside, sitting in the truck bed, his turn to sleep—he spent a lot of energy trouncing Matthews in football the night before, his new limbs working double time. Fred, the nonsmoker, works a toothpick between his lips.

You've got the Taj Mahal in toothpicks inside your gut, says Hump. I heard about one at the World's Fair. The toothpick part, not your stomach.

I'm not nervous, says Fred. I enjoy my work.

Matthews chews on the bread that is his breakfast. He has been silent all the way out here, something chewing on him, and not his football loss because that's steady.

Hump holds his match up to the wind at the window crack to blow it out but the wind just blows it away. He is waiting waiting waiting for his girl's decision. She has to take him seriously this time.

They think the problem with the shell was lousy packing, says Matthews.

You said the kid was in boot camp? asks Fred.

Never got to the front. He was my nephew, says Matthews. Kin.

Hump fills the cab with smoke. The Krauts come at you and damn, you don't know what to do. They have to practice, says Hump. I had a dream I didn't.

I'm not arguing with you, says Matthews. He jams his crust into the cigarette tray. It's a terrible thing when anybody gets it. But to have it happen to him.

They all stare out at the tumbleweed-dotted windy plains. He was your sister's kid? says Hump.

Matthews nods. She signed him up just to make a point with me. Somebody in the family has to do something, she said.

We'll just check the shells better ourselves, says Fred. Right? Right?

Right, they say.

Bang! they all jump.

It's Otto outside, holding the shreds of a paper bag, a big grin across his no-good face.

Son of a gun, says Fred, who starts laughing. Hell's afire.

Don't do that, Matthews shouts at Otto, rubbing the top of his head where he hit the roof. Don't ever do that again.

Hump rolls down his window. The lieutenant won't let Matthews off for the funeral.

Otto raises his eyebrows by way of *Too bad,* and hooks his armpits over the window hole, blocking the wind a little. He's saving the sorting for him, or the women.

Matthews glares.

I saw a notice on the board outside the bathroom, says Fred, tucking his half-finished toothpick into his pressed pocket. Don't you ever read?

I read literature, says Hump. In the bathroom.

Matthews snorts. Why did I get a college degree?

We have to show the army bean counters where we put everything, says Fred. They want a map because they need new places to bury stuff. The igloos are already almost full up and the war isn't even half over. Or so they say.

How're we going to come up with a map? says Hump. The shingles have pretty much blown away. This is real wind.

Fred lowers his forehead to the steering wheel. We have to protect people.

Will you shut up? says Hump. Half the time the turkeys blast off in another direction entirely.

I am going to find them all, says Matthews. I know it. I'll be walking along and there they will be. At least I'll be protecting civilians.

You are the historical one after all, says Fred. You like things written down.

Hysterical one, mutters Otto.

Matthews just glares some more, he's that tense, trying to keep from getting into a fight.

They squint out the side window where the antelope have come again to roam. I wouldn't go there if I were them, says Hump. It's for sure on the map.

But the antelope make it all the way over the horizon.

You can find some of the ordnance with those machines that you pick up money from a beach with, says Fred. I read about those in *Popular Mechanics*.

Otto straightens his mended legs in an exercise, barely holding onto the window edge. They'll put us under arrest, he says. When they find out what we did.

They will not, says Matthews. I know about arrests.

Otto imitates a siren, then moves his cigarette into the cab where it won't blow out. Pacifist! He puffs. The smoke billows on the *p*. We are fighting just the same by fixing up the bombs. We're the real flag wavers.

Matthews turns his face away from the smoke. Mustard gas isn't the only thing that makes him sick. Like hell, he says.

Lay off, says Fred. You two.

Nobody cared much about what we did with the bombs back then as long as we did it is what I recall, says Hump. That lieutenant sure didn't. Duds for the duds.

You've been a lost case ever since you met that girl, says Matthews.

I have not, says Hump. I just need another cigarette. He holds his fingers in a *v* for a puff of Otto's.

Matthews rolls down his window, wind or no wind, and vomits.

Matthews decides he would rather go to jail than repair another bomb. He starts going around at work with play handcuffs hooked to his overalls. Just to make a point, he tells them, just to show them what's really going on, how people who disagree with the government in a democracy can get imprisoned for their so-called free speech. He will write a book about it in jail where he can finally get some peace and quiet. He carries on like that for a week, hoping to be arrested, but nobody takes the bait. Otto says it is Matthews's Last Stand. He and Matthews have been quarreling over tent space, and Matthews has to struggle to keep his temper over that and all the rest, every night getting his anger out playing more football. There he runs after Otto like a wild man, throwing the ball high, running out to the goal and back for nothing, warmed up and ferocious.

Officer Matthews, Hump says in short gulps of air from running so hard, please hand over that ball.

You never throw it to me, complains Matthews, giving it up. None of you.

You're just too old, says Otto, dancing around the two of them. You're too historical.

Fred calms Matthews down, says this is a game with rules, this is his chance to break them.

Hump plays in a daze, handicapped as he is in the girl way, now three weeks into waiting for her decision. They all offer solace, yes they do, all day, because they like to see him mad, and then they don't, they feel sorry for him because when a girl goes home to think they all know what that means. Even his mother is suspicious, though he tells her nothing relevant, he just burns up the field with his halfback charge. Only Fred rivals him. The doctor said the service wouldn't be good for me, says Fred, who moans and clutches his pocket over his heart region, then steals the ball right out from under Hump. Matthews laughs and tackles him anyway.

You're not so bad at defense for being such an offensive guy, says Hump.

Matthews rattles his handcuffs.

The local girls who wander over—why would they play without girls watching?—sing fight songs that make them play even harder and longer, right into the mud, this being the muddiest spring ever. Hump drags himself soaking out of a pile and sees his girl cheering with the others. She must've driven all this way to talk to him, no *Dear John* for her. He waves but he can't exactly quit in the middle of the game to hear what she has to say, he would be razzed forever. Instead he makes a big show of trotting into place in his warrior outfit, shoving at the shoulder pads they've begged from the high school, grinning at her under his mouse-ear helmet through all the mud on his face. His legs go jelly though, all nerves, he even glances down at the mud to see if that is the problem.

Not so far away, somebody on the next shift is testing artillery to see if the lot is good, the explosives booming *yes*. Hump had that shift a few days before. It was fun, lofting the ammo as high as you could, and you could still see the game. Like dropping apples in a basket, says Otto. Puts me right to sleep, he says, in the huddle. Matthews says he'll wake him up, and in the next play, he throws himself around Otto's legs and brings him down with a good thump. A couple of minutes later one of the gun struts collapses from the thrust of the mortar. None of the football players know about that, they are already running a fancy Hail Mary play, Hump in the lead with a squirt of speed pure show-off. The shell gets lobbed anyway and goes south.

Matthews! shouts Fred, and Matthews turns around with his arms curled like that because he thinks Fred for once is throwing him the ball the way he is supposed to.

Run over by a truck reads the report.

She says yes. She has driven all this way to say no despite her waking at night, sure he breathed beside her, despite his post-card *Love is for the birds,* its two geese taking off together, signed with his real name, despite her father's opinion either way. She says yes that night after she'd washed her skirt several times in the PX sink to remove a smear of flesh, a sheet wrapped around her for modesty, after the ambulance scraped up what was left while they embraced, the mud on Hump's face thinning with tears, after they stood as still as chess pieces with the flesh raining down, after Fred's terrible scream, because she thinks—she is sure, she has to—that she can keep Hump safe.

I'll keep an eye on the works, she tells her father. It is her final selling point. Sticking point, he pronounces it after he calls in her mother, waiting in the dining room for news of the daugh-ter-father summit. Despite her ill-timed pacifist remarks, he's won another term, and maybe he can corner that part of the state with her in it for the next one. He doesn't tell her that, but he also doesn't say the plant is not safe, he campaigned that it was safe, that's how it got to be built. It's been safe so far, he tells her mother. Those old bombs are harmless. A few accidents, but they happen in any factory.

This is not to say that her mother doesn't invoke class, the boy's unsuitable station in life, all the other beaus with money, the depot's bad water, how she is wasting her diploma, and the economic instability of his chosen industry.

Margaret wooden-legs the conversation: running for political office isn't so dependable. Besides, she says, there's all my other sisters.

They extend what congratulations they can.

Father loves you best because you have his hair, says her sister closest in age, combing Margaret's long curls fancy before the wedding.

I am surprised he's so agreeable, she says, staring into the mirror.

Her sister fixes a bobby pin between her teeth. It's never fair, is it? I mean, look at me—piecemeal, I ought to be a pet of them both, mom's legs, mom's skin, dad's nose, dad's hands. It's just my girliness that tips it opposite in each category.

You have your own self. She's not looking in the mirror but at her sister, who smiles.

You are just like him, always saying what will make people happy. Her sister arranges her own curls but they spring up, they poke out.

She smooths her sister's hair. Get yourself a beau and it won't matter.

Oh, bow tie, she says. You've got muffin crumbs on your front.

She doesn't fall for it, she doesn't look down to check so her sister can snip her nose.

I worry you won't like the small-town life, says her sister, picking up the comb again.

Maybe, maybe not—but I'll try to do something about it. She gives her hair two pushes with the heel of her hand until it settles into place. There, she says. I'm fixed.

The wedding is a half-inch in the capital newspaper. It runs longer in Igloo's, but is noted with puzzlement on the state radio's *Hitching Post* because the services aren't held at home amongst the bowers of legislative significance but in Hump's mother's backyard and porch. The mother is housebound is Margaret's father's excuse to avoid the politically awkward possibilities, and his mother accepts this with the greed of no other wedding party ever again. Margaret is given away amongst this year's new peonies and her unmarried sisters, no one too overdressed except in sheer number, and her mother wearing a big purple brooch in competition with her daughter's glory. But the bride wins, and wins again, the way brides have to, a good fit in her mother's old satin, lace, and veil. Hump himself looks movie-star sharp in a suit his own father left behind, and there are college girls everywhere, flirting because where else are they going to see so many men? telling all the workers how important they are to the war. Even the girl truck drivers show up.

One of those girl truck drivers circles Fred, has for some time. She follows him down the reception line, where he takes the bride's hand. It's a sad, sad day for so many, he says. He looks over at Hump and shakes his head.

Don't be shy, says Hump. Every one of my old flames came. They won't eat you.

The girl truck driver titters.

Fred bares his teeth. I know what they like, I just don't always give it to them.

I'm shocked, says the bride. Such a big bad wolf.

Fred snaps at a sandwich being passed instead of the girl.

Pictures, pictures, interrupts Hump's mother, rolling into the room.

The one-armed photographer does the honors, the priest holding up his missal in the middle, both families arranged in graded rows around him, with the bride and groom at the bottom. His mother has herself wheeled next to her son, who puts his hand on her shoulder. She's green-sheathed, with a fancy corsage tied to her wrist made of corn stalks. For fertility she tells everyone, to start them blushing. High color makes for a good portrait, she insists.

Next, the groom's guys decide to make a pyramid, shoes to shoulders, and the photographer doesn't stop them, terror and laughter at war on their faces while Hump teeters on top, his blond hair perfectly parted and affixed to his head with hair cream, his father's old suit flapped open to show where it is basted to fit.

Otto is standing close when the garter's thrown, he almost catches it on a whoop, his uplifted arm like a horseshoe post, but it lands in Fred's lap. He stands up so quick it hits the floor and has to be tossed again.

Six months later everyone moves into Igloo. By then even Otto has found a wife, even Fred has run off to the preacher's with that thick-haunched truck driver, even he gets a little house in amongst all the other newly built matching houses, with matching rabbit hutches. In no time at all, all these matching men go in and kiss the wrong wives. Well, Fred does once, in the dark and more than half drunk. The woman involved was actually Hump, who was turned to his washer, listening to a loose bolt bang, bent over with his hair wet from the shower in the dark, or so Fred said later. His trucker wife is the cheerful sort, she just giggled and said it could have been worse, it could have been Hump's ma.

She doesn't move in with them. She orders this new wheelchair out of aluminum and soon scoots around her house like a bug. They invite her over to warm up their new place. She brings bread fresh out of the oven from a neighbor who has two kids and says they won't grow up right with Wonder Bread, it's I-wonder-bread to her. Otto has killed an antelope in the artillery range and has presented them with steaks. There's also vegetables.

Margaret stirs a sauce at the stove, wearing an apron her mother gave her. She's never worn one before, having always had maids. A kind of tingly sensation of captivity thrills her, she tells him when he ties it around her waist, yanking at its bow. She can just see herself in the hall mirror and it looks like a half slip showing off over her skirt, it is that flouncy. Exciting? she says with her hip out. With his mother looking for her glasses, Hump pinches her backside with a *yes*.

Losing her glasses at her age—you're not so old, says Hump—means you might as well be cooking mush. Three-fourths of taste is sight, she says. But it all certainly smells good. She rolls herself out of the kitchen in her new chair with vigor.

Hump's setting the table with odds and ends. Their fancy set remains enshrined in the closet with the Swedish kerchiefs Margaret bought at their honeymoon town about twenty miles away. They even had Swedish pancakes for dinner, Hump's telling his mother. She accepts the orange slice he hands her as a sort of foreign appetizer, all the way from California, a good place to retire. No, I'd never move, she's saying, your father wouldn't be able to find me, if he ever thought about coming back. With the war done and the munitions coming back, we're all going to be happy here.

Hump loves her and loves her. Desire is all over him, his feet swell, his throat catches, he doesn't know what to do with his hands when they're not on her. They even go down to the train station once in a historical reenactment. At work the men see how love-haggard he is all the time, and occasionally it kindles actual sympathy instead of jokes. They all offer to help, yes they do, on a regular basis. A fair number of their wives have lost their babies and envy the possibility of hers. These women have started joining the men at work, the truck girls have been demoted to sorting or capping with them, what they did for pin money in high school they do now for real, with nothing at home to stop them. They sit in a room in hairnets and fish out parts while the guys ride around in their vehicles, whistling or cursing, showing off, laying down a culvert to keep the poisons draining during the rains or unloading junk bits from New Mexico, stuff from bombs that has stood around so long it is only good for grinding or burying. A couple of the women do have kids but they're so sickly they can't be left alone a minute or their mothers find them worse. The other women take up a collection for a full-time sitter, they don't want to hear a baby cry in a bassinet next to their desks, it makes them cry. Otto's wife—a big girl who carries big—is like that. But nobody thinks about moving. Igloo is a sort of prairie utopia, all races together, there's even a black man who grades the roads, everybody's getting a piece of the postwar action.

Your water's red, Hump says, taking the opportunity himself outside the shed where the wind isn't too bad.

What about it? says Fred, zipping up. He hasn't said *Boo* to Hump since he made his kissing mistake.

It looks like you've been eating beets all winter.

None of your business what I eat, says Fred.

If you're going to be touchy, says Hump.

They are back inside the shed, mulling over what to do with a crate of mustard gas because it's raining and nothing gets blown off when it's raining. Somebody relates a story about a rabbit somebody hit with a truck—just a tap—and then handed it into the office thinking he could get on sick leave.

There won't be no brass band nor pension for me, says Fred, under cover of all the rabbit story laughter. Like Matthews. If what the doc says is true.

Doc's not always right, says Hump. He told me not to smoke, and look at me, fit as a fiddle. Hump thumps his overall-covered chest.

I don't know what to think, says Fred. My girl guesses it's why I'm not so interested in her.

Hump has nothing to say on that point. Maybe you should find a doc who'll tell you something different.

They are both bending their heads a little toward their crotches when Otto comes in, dragging a piece of tin and a radio report.

They're at it in Korea, says Otto.

All the men in the room go quiet. They can just hear the radio being turned up in the next shed, but barely.

Whoever's safe? she says to Hump in the dark after he hits the pillow, after he bunches it up and closes his eyes.

No one, except your father, so happy with his H-bomb.

She sighs, she licks the tip of his ear. Mmmmmm, she says, it's all the way into your ear canal. Tastes sweet.

He practically purrs. They mix it with sugar so the cakes hold together.

She sits back. You're not allowed to tell me that.

You think the army's got paper cups to our bedroom walls?

She doles out pills for the cough he can't get over. You poor husky boys need your vitamins. All that fresh air and exercise can't be good for you. She caps the container while he snakes his arm around her and gets the light.

I'm reading, she says, and snaps it back on.

More Shakespeare? He bunches his pillow, closing his eyes.

The one about the old father and the girls, she says. The father's not happy.

Fred said he heard his neighbor bitch about him talking in his sleep—through the wall, he says. We should give him something to listen to.

You never talk anymore, she says, not even in your sleep.

I'm a fast talker, he says, and you know it. He lights her cigarette, a habit she has in bed.

What does that make me? she says. A fast listener? I am going to do something about us, she says, exhaling. I am going to buy some of that land next to the depot and find out the whys of everything.

He opens his eyes. You shouldn't waste a nickel on it.

It's the only way to find out what's what. This is a company town.

He throws his arm over her chest and taps her nipple.

No, you are not changing the subject, she says. A little lop-sided piece of a quarter section is coming up for auction. It's not expensive—who wants their cows close to the depot when the big trucks scare them? I'll just let the grass grow. I'll use dad's wedding money.

No money, honey, he says. I bought the new appliances with it, he says.

There's a big enough silence that he can actually hear her tears drop. She is stirred up by being so pregnant, she is over-concerned with his cough, and Fred being sick, and maybe nervous.

Oh, honey, he says. Maybe my mother can loan us something.

It is Hump's day off and he is helping the refrigerator man, steadying the tipping end of the appliance, with a cup of coffee in his other hand. He was up too late the night before, her arguing that she loved him too much to let him wear those pants one more time, and him calming her down, of course he'll find something else, and they ended up making love for one more sweet hour. She answers the phone in the bedroom while he eases the appliance into place, thanks to the workman's two-step maneuvering.

It is one of the igloos again, she says through the crack in the door.

Nobody wants a jumpy fire, one that warms up the other igloos. Fred and Otto and Hump are the experts at cooling them. They have handled the most turkeys, are always the first to handle them. What are they doing, still holding on to them anyway? says Fred when Hump shows up at his door, honking.

They've got some kind of romance going, says Hump.

You're the one with romance, says Fred, as Hump gets into the car. It's that turkeys make the lieutenant feel he's still a big shot.

Hump agrees by gulping the rest of his coffee.

Otto is waving at the base of the igloo in question, antsy in any emergency, something explosive they haven't set for themselves. There's a bomb inside that's as hot as a pinup, he says. Smoke signals.

They stare at the pipe sticking out of the igloo, its heat a cloud of condensation that someone noticed, driving by.

All right, then, says Fred after he jerks its steel door open. Let's lay out the hoses. Whose turn is it to take on the ladder?

The bombs are laid on their sides in rows and it looks as if the problem is near the top.

They draw straws and Hump picks the short one.

It is kind of his fault anyway, his wife's father voting the place in, and the guy voted funds for the war in the first place, and it is Hump's fault too that his handsomeness attracted the daughter, his fault they have their jobs and houses and lots of other crazy notions they don't need to talk about, they just have him deal with problems like this as often as they can. Nobody says they fix the straws that they draw. They were all happy enough to blow these turkeys when they first arrived in the depot but now when they turn iffy in these igloos—well, Hump is almost always best suited for the repair job, he's now the expert.

He never says, Let's draw again. Besides, Fred can't go up the ladder so easily anymore, he's not so agile, something the doc told him would start to happen. But he can plug in and tune the radio. He turns it up loud so the Lindy can loosen Hump up, it makes him liable to jump onto the ladder "like an Eskimono," the way Hump yells it, giving his bottom a little shake.

Skinnying up the ladder, Hump feels the angry hot of the shell, its *Let's see what you pussies can do about this.* Otto is holding the ladder. He has not had but a drop or two of booze before the call. It is not as if he isn't happy with his marital state, his new little boy, a brave he says, the bravest. A drop or two in winter wets down the cabin fever, the teepee fever, he tells Fred. *Gesundheit!* he says, his only word in German.

On top now, Hump pulls up a mask and roars with bravery, clips his leg to the frame and beats his chest to the radio.

We haven't got all day, says Fred, who finds a cigarette, a brand new habit.

Otto screams at him. Fred already has it in his mouth. Okay, okay, he says, and throws the cigarette to the ground.

It has not been lit.

Otto turns off the radio.

Hump fiddles with the shells in the cold silence after that, the way he has for the last two years of fiddling, he doesn't even turn around to see what they are so worked up about, he doesn't turn at all so they never see his sudden look of surprise.

She's combing her hair in the mirror over the sink, wondering about baby names, and nicknames, a dreamy stare-at-your-nose that she's about to turn away from, hearing the washer finish, when *Boom!* the porcelain turns pink from the explosion.

She has the baby on the day of the funeral. The shock of it all, people say. Although Fred is dead too, his wife taking the first bus out with his pension, it is Hump gone they can't stop shaking their heads over. Hump, the handsome hero. They nearly forget about Otto. It takes them a whole day to dig him out, the top of the igloo blowing straight up in the air then all that cement crashing down on the insides.

I thought I was done for, Otto tells the reporter from his hospital bed. I saw a flash of flame and it was like looking into a furnace. I never did hear any explosion, just a bright light. I was buried from the hips down.

He lies in the hospital for a month. It is right after he is discharged, still with a cast on one arm, that he visits her. He presents her with a fetish of arrowhead and grass and rabbit fur that she hangs over the bureau, next to Hump's mother's cornstalk cross, two angry twists. Standing in her living room beside the baby asleep in his crib, he whispers that Hump wasn't one to give up or shirk, and takes off his hat. Inside its cup lie his two braids, cut from his head. Matthews too, he says, and hands them to her.

The hair is two heavy ropes, warm from the top of his head, the truncated ends a chopped piece of him. She can't look up because of what she hears. When she does, she takes a step closer and puts her arms around him.

They just stand there.

OGALLALA AQUIFER

Buffalo harrumph. You don't have to stand too close and you can still hear them. On a good day if you've got one of those buffalo nickels in your pocket, they can see it and will come at you for it, try to take it right out of that pocket. This one comes from South Dakota. That's the last place left where buffalos are bred.

His grandfather knows buffalo, his grandfather makes sure the boy knows too. His mother has just moved back from the East Coast, and the boy doesn't know anything about here, buffalo or not. Take the boy around, she told him. It's his land someday too.

The boy doesn't care about buffalo or even the buffalo nickels that his grandfather produces out of a slot in the air vent. All he cares about in this heat is ice cream. His grandfather treated him at a shop so many miles behind them that the chocolate cone he holds is almost finished. Now his grandfather has stopped the pickup to look at this buffalo he's keeping for his neighbor. The wind is tearing at its ruff and beard and from the pickup, the boy can see its piss change to spray as it turns to look at them.

We have owned this parcel for fifty-two years, his grandfather says. I don't know if you realize how long a period of time that is. To me it was just yesterday that I bought it, I remember the papers and the scratchy sound of the fountain pen.

What's a fountain pen? asks the boy.

His grandfather laughs and drives slowly on. There's sugar beets coming up, he points out the window past the boy's nose. There's a big stand of rye in with that corn there, which I will show you how to pull out.

The boy stretches his neck to watch the buffalo behind him walk down the fallen dead cornstalk row, he watches until there's just the buffalo head sticking up. Mom says buffalo plowed up the grass even before the Indians came and kept it green.

Well, that is true, just like your mama says. An environmental help would be how she would put it. See that fence post to the east? He sweeps his arm out over the boy's head. There was no fence there when I bought it, none whatsoever for fifty miles. That's the way the buffalo liked it. That way you get your greener grass, no problem. Let's have a look at that fence, see if it's having any trouble holding him. You afraid?

The boy snaps his seatbelt free, the question not worth an answer. They park and his grandfather puts his hand on the boy's shoulder for support when they duck under the barbed wire, then they head across the field. The boy resists turning around to see if the buffalo is following them. They are halfway across when his grandfather stops. This is good soil, he says. He kicks at a clump of dirt left in a tractor track. This is about the best soil there is.

The boy looks at the dirt.

You don't know good dirt when you see it? says his grandfather. We feed the U. S. of A. and half the rest of the world with this dirt. And do you know our secret? Do you see any rivers around here?

The boy looks out on the wind blowing the grass half over, wavy like a river itself. No, he says as if he has thought about it.

There's water underneath your feet here, everywhere.

There is not, says the boy.

Can't you feel it? Strong old water. Prehistoric. A huge amount, about the biggest amount of water in the world is trapped in this underground gravel. They call it an aquifer.

Thirst rushes into the boy for something wet and old, like Coke.

Come on, says his grandfather. I can see from here that fence is fine. You wouldn't believe me about the water if a lake jumped up out of the ground and bit you.

The boy dodges the old man's pinch. He can feel the buffalo watch them in their retreat.

Getting into the pickup, the grandfather says, You drive. I'll work the pedals. The boy sticks his neck up high, over the wheel. There's the ditch, says his grandfather. You don't want to drive there.

The boy steers the pickup along the gravel road until they spot a big cloud of dust in the distance. What's that? says the boy.

Don't get excited, says his grandfather, his hand crossing the boy's chest to the wheel. We've got to check that field anyway.

The boy lifts the chain off the fence post while his grandfather drives the pickup through the gate, shouting out the window to catch some of the plastic bags flying around in the dust, and to stick them under the tire in the back of the pickup.

He misses two. No grocery store around here, he says, climbing back into his seat. Where do all those bags come from?

Heaven, says his grandfather. He squints down the road. That's more than one car's worth of kickup, that's a lot of dust—is it a funeral procession? What do you think?

They're not cars, says the boy.

His grandfather leans forward and sees that the boy's right, they're huge dump trucks with heavy loads tarped down good except for one, the grandfather says as they approach the edge of his land, he can almost see underneath the blowing tarp as the truck rumbles close, closer, as they all pass them. Out-of-state plates, says the grandfather.

The boy counts at least a hundred of them, and he starts counting right away. Then all a hundred or so trucks don't disappear, taking their dirt cloud with them, they turn off at the next crossroad and stop a half mile away where there's a hill.

Dust gets inside the pickup despite the windows being rolled. His grandfather takes off his cap and wipes his face. It's the dump they've gone to, where it borders my land, he says.

The boy fiddles with a lever and dust blows out from the vents.

Cut that out, says his grandfather.

His grandfather takes over driving, turning into the facility with all the time in the world, cruising right past the big *Waste Management, Enjoy!* sign at the gate. Big enough to welcome them to the biggest mountain in the three-state area, made big like that by one of the fastest growing corporations in the world, which is the first thing Will, the operator, likes to make clear if you so much as breathe in his direction, the grandfather says to the boy. Unless he's been on some corporate junket that these dumps put on, one of those shaking-hands conferences Will likes to talk about best.

He drives slow beside the trucks lined up to be weighed. A blast of wind blows a dust devil of dirt, paper, and plastic from the garbage pit behind them onto the fence line. He tells his grandson he has filed a complaint against Waste Management about it. He's got a law degree and finds that useful now and then. It's his cows that get mouthfuls of paper, balls of plastic in their bowels. Paper and trash cover his crop, stick in his machines. On top of that, his plants get dirty from all the blow-off and don't grow. It's a long argument that the wind doesn't help, especially this time of year, especially now, with all those dump trucks. In the middle of their settling dust, Will walks over to meet them. He's got looks a girl would start a rosary for, a goatee just the right size, and a big friendly-looking collie dog.

Vegas was great, says Will. Thank you for asking. The corporation paid for everything. Now what can I do for you today?

I was just going to show my grandson what a dump is all about, says the grandfather.

You don't want your old swing set rusting in your backyard until kingdom come? Will leans into the boy's window, his big smile ready to go. We take that and any of your old telephone books your gramps doesn't have a place for, or say there's a gas station that closes up—we go in and scrape out the bad dirt from under it so you can build a new daycare center or a school right on top of it.

Pretty good, says the grandfather. You should do Rotary.

I have, says Will.

So, what's going on?

Will resettles his cap. The usual, he says. Just more of it.

The trucks have South Dakota plates. Pretty strange, he says. To be hauling trash five hundred miles.

We've got almost a thousand or so trucks coming, Will says. His dog wags at his cheerful tone. We have them staggered so a convoy of them arrives every four hours. That way we won't disturb the neighbors much.

His grandfather watches the dump trucks empty: dirt, dirt, dirt. We are your closest neighbors, Will, he says. You shouldn't keep secrets from us. It's not just dirt in those trucks. If it were, I'd take some.

Will shoves his hands into his jeans, his head bent. He gives his dog the eye from under his cap. This is a private corporation, he says. Under the terms of this contract, I've already said too much about it. I'm sorry.

His grandfather just lets that sit between them. The boy watches the garbage whirl itself out.

Okay, I'll get my crew on that fence first thing, just as soon as I get this first batch of trucks dumped out, Will promises.

A thousand trucks! his grandfather says. A damned wagon train. I'm not happy about it.

He lifts a hand to Will by way of a brusque goodbye and drives out. What did you see? he asks the boy.

Dirt, says the boy. Nothing but dirt in those trucks.

A mile from the dump mountain, the newspaper girl waves at them from her truck, stopped at the intersection.

Newspaper woman, says the boy after the grandfather makes the identification.

So your mother says. His grandfather smiles.

The newspaper girl has her turn signal on and her two kids strapped into seats beside her. His grandfather honks and pulls close alongside.

The dust is still so bad she hesitates to roll down her window. Makes me want to move, she shouts through the crack.

You know what's going on?

I'm calling people, she says. Who puts that much dirt in a dump?

Unless there's money in it, he says.

Money in dirt? the boy wonders. He crunches grit between his teeth, remembering ice cream.

Your mother will say no, says his grandfather. She likes to put a stop to things. He is smoking while he drives home, something he hardly ever does, tipping the ash into a coffee-ringed Styrofoam cup. Although she didn't say no soon enough in the case of her job, he says. Her own office was bad. From what she tells me, they had printers spraying poison and roof tar coming in through the air vents and no windows that opened. Can you imagine that? A government office in Washington, DC, with a mandate to protect the whole country's environment operating day after day without any air?

He knows by now his grandfather doesn't need an answer.

Now here there's nothing in our air, says his grandfather. Go ahead, stick your nose out into it. He rolls down his window and his grandson's, and the boy gets a lungful.

From working in that office, she does know a little more than most folks here do about what is supposed to go into the land, at least legally speaking, says his grandfather, dropping his butt out the window and rolling both of theirs up again. And she knows what she knows from cell level too: she says her joints ache whenever there's roof-tarring now or a crop-dusting, and her throat closes up if someone's wearing dry cleaning too close to her, what drove that husband of hers into divorce court he says, pulling into the drive, but not—he seems to think—so the boy can hear.

I've got your first case, he says to her, walking in.

I haven't been here two weeks, she says. She is at the kitchen computer, scouring for jobs, and coughs at the waft of gasoline the boy brings in behind him. You filled your grandad's pickup again?

Sorry, says her father. He likes doing it. I forget.

Go take a shower, she tells the boy. He whines, he stalls, she takes an air-swat at his behind, she coughs again, he concedes.

Her father fills her in while she tosses leftovers into a pot.

Tarps? she says. Why do they need to cover dirt?

Blows around. He rubs his eyes under his glasses.

There'll be a couple of other people with property around there wondering about all those trucks, she says. It's not going to be just you.

He harrumphs. She took up law because of him and his lawyering but by the time she graduated, he'd quit his practice to farm full time. See where fooling around with the law got her—sick. He's not all that well either, really, and surely he can't see so perfectly—a thousand of those trucks! Nearly put him to sleep listening to the boy count.

Soon all three knife and fork their way through dinner. Did your grandfather show you every single pasture? she asks the boy.

The boy is telling her about the ice cream when the phone rings.

It's the newspaper girl.

He puts up his hearing aid. The newspaper girl wants him to know it's a government thing, that somebody's ordered the move.

They were driving around in broad daylight so I guess so, he says. But I don't like it.

I don't like it either, says the newspaper girl. My property's just about as close as yours. Watch the TV tonight, she says. The station called to get background so I know they're doing a story.

His daughter puts their dishes in the dishwasher. He pours in the soap because it gives her hives to be next to the stuff, humoring her. No doubt she thinks she's doing him a favor by coming home to housekeep, it isn't all just about the clean air. He makes some tea, which she refuses. She won't sleep with its caffeine, it's hard enough to sleep anyway, with all that who-knows-what coming.

You know who has to know something? she says, drying her hands on a dishtowel. The DEQ.

You and your environmental people, he says, searching for sugar.

Mine? At EPA we used to call them the Department of Environmental Questions, not Quality. But they would have to know because it's their job and it's interstate. You can't move that much waste from one state to another without permits.

They like to keep their mouths shut, that much I know, he says. But the county commissioners—they might be able to help you.

She quiets the boy's zombie-killing game on the computer to catch the local TV station's piece on the cavalcade of trucks, including footage of Will waving them in. The announcer jokes that South Dakota has so much land they have to get rid of it. Then he says the dirt's from an old munitions processing plant that's slated to sell. So many trucks coming, he says, the dust plume can be seen by satellite. Everyone in the country can see the next hundred trucks on their way. All truckloads altogether—sixty thousand tons of dirt.

Her father lets his tea get cold, he is that upset.

The county commissioners like to meet early, before eight a.m. That's not what the once-a-week schedule says, it says 8:30 as if it were writ in stone, but he knows better. Farmers are wont to be outside working every daylight minute this time of year, they have to meet early. He leaves for the meeting just as his daughter and her son are using the bathroom. Six overalled men fill the thirties' Depression chairs the courthouse started with, and Deaver, the skinny implements man, sitting at the head, looks as if he hasn't eaten since.

The newspaper girl doesn't take a seat at the table, she's half on her phone all the time, she's in and out.

By 8:40 it's time for public input, and he stands and asks what's going on at the dump. It's not right, whatever this company is doing so secretly. It's our water underneath.

All the sidewalk-contracting, pothole-governing, sanitation-inspecting business of commissioners hasn't prepared them for investigations. The commissioners shake their heads, they scratch them. The first I heard about it was on TV last night, says Deaver, palms up on the scarred meeting table. What's so wrong with it?

I'm sure it's fine, says the bald guy next to him.

The grandfather sits back in his chair. Really? You have to recuse yourself anyway, don't you? It'd be a conflict of interest with your investment in the dump.

I have a little money in it, he says, passing his hands over his bare head as if to cover it. Not especially in this transport.

I wondered how the dump got opened so fast, says the man in a red ball cap across from him. That's real interesting.

What about contacting the governor? asks the grandfather before things get out of hand. He's the one who ought to deal with these jokers. Interstate is his job.

The newspaper girl takes a note.

The commissioners aren't happy about being the ones to contact the governor. That's a big question, says Deaver. I've got land to plow this morning—let's put it on next week's agenda.

The bald guy nods.

All of the dirt will be dumped by then, the grandfather says. He looks at his watch. Six hundred more trucks coming pronto.

The newspaper girl gives him a thumbs up, but the men file out.

At least you got them thinking, says his daughter when he shows up for lunch. She practically claps.

I drove by the dump to check on their progress. I've got dust all over me.

She steps way back from him but she's still beaming. I'm looking into Waste Management. If I find stuff we can use, we could take out an ad on the radio and let people know what's going on, schedule a demonstration at the courthouse.

He looks at her as if she has grown a third arm, he nods but slowly. I suppose we could. Where's that grandson of mine?

It's a school day, have you forgotten? She stirs a pot. Everybody should know what's in their water. It is a democracy.

He sticks his hand into the pile of the morning's newspapers and pulls a random sheet up to his face to inspect. He nods again but this time it's as if he's absorbed in a very interesting article.

I can use a lot of what I've learned from the government sector, she says, ladling out lunch from the pot. We could work out a class action suit.

He folds the paper back into its rectangles.

I suppose it's not exactly a good thing to have this kind of work again, she says, putting lunch on the table. I thought I was safe here. The environment here was so clean—that was the whole point of my moving home. It's about the last place left.

He eyes the green stuff in his soup. Kale.

Want to split a beer? she says. If you have a whole one, you'll sleep all afternoon.

He says he'll take what he can get.

Eyes shifty inside a lean face—Will's a serial-killer type, she decides, even with *Volvo* across his ball cap. Cute though, with that funny goatee.

I just want to see what you're doing about all those bags flying onto his place, she says, letting her motor run. Our place, she says.

Right this way, says Will, with a little bow. Let me give you the grand tour.

She smiles her just-divorced smile back at him, she can't help herself, she parks, and takes a seat in his truck. They drive up a road spiraling up the side of the mountain, wheat brushing the side of the car where he's planted it to hold down the fill.

It reminds me of where the Native Americans put their trash, she says. A midden, they call it. There was always a big hill of it outside each village.

So it's kind of like a historical monument, he says. It's a good thing, his hands gesture.

I wouldn't go so far as to say that. Nobody remembers what even the ground around here used to look like, she says, with the rabbits and creeks and all the different grasses.

Like over past the dry creek bed where the government pays you to keep it like that?

Pretty much, she says.

At the top she gets out and walks away from where he's headed, as if she's lost just leaving the car, and there they are: six huge new mounds of dirt right up next to a mess of old Roundup barrels, creosote railroad ties, and a heap of bright colored plastic who-knows-what. The new mounds are not covered.

Wrong way, he says. Over here, he waves. Let me show you.

Okay, she says. She's seen enough already.

What we have here is a state-of-the-art facility, he boasts, and the biggest one in six counties. You can see all the way into Colorado, he says, directing her to look out over her father's farm, past the plastic-bag-and-trash-blown fence that is eight foot high. Where we catch most of what there is.

That's important to my dad. He keeps picking it up.

I have the retarded working on it too. An after-school program. He points down at a hodgepodge group—boys, girls, adults—who are coming around the side of the hill picking up the trash along the face of the fence. They make good money, he says. Some of the families need it.

A big gust of wind rains dust at them.

Really—what a great job you're doing, she says, trying to swallow as little of the dust as possible.

We even have a federal permit, he says, folding his arms over his chest. We got it last year. It says we're allowed to take stuff ten percent more toxic than the limit. That really opens things up for us.

Before her silence gets overly eloquent, she points at a pink puddle near the bottom of the mountain.

That? he says. After it evaporates we put the soil in drums and bury it. All with the latest tech.

Bulldozers? she says.

That would be it, he says, with not quite the enthusiasm he had before, a little annoyed, recognizing that she might be picking on him.

I am so grateful for your time, she says, and he brightens, then they get back into his pickup and he drives back down. She keeps coughing, which makes it hard for her to answer any questions about herself.

At the bottom he turns the pickup toward his work shed. It could be an outhouse it is so small but it has an other-purpose look to it, lacy curtains against the one window. One of the trash-picking kids sucks his dirty thumb at the door, and then—before they are quite parked—another boy joins hands with him. They run up the side of the hill, catching the loose papers between their arms, the rest slapping their legs. At the top, two others link with them, backlit, moving in a kind of dance across the top of the mountain.

I've seen that in a movie, she says, after he turns off the ignition.

Foreign, I'll bet, says Will.

The Seventh Seal.

Will ducks his head in a kind of *yes,* as if he knew the title all along. Hey, he says, you want to see our monthly reports?

They show all our efforts to date, he says. He slaps his dusty jeans and she takes that for *Okay, let's,* and they go right inside.

His collie dog hams it up after they walk in, sniffs her crotch and begs for a cookie.

There, he says, producing a cookie and a spiral-bound notebook from inside a drawer. A ballpoint pen holds the place where it falls open. See here, he says. Do you know we actually close this operation if the wind blows over forty miles per hour?

She's lazy about her eyes, she doesn't look down at the numbers, she looks right at him. What's the difference in dust between thirty and forty miles per hour? Any way you look at that, it's a lot of wind, and possible poison blowing a long way. Tell me, she says, all that new waste you have on the other side is going to be buried, isn't it?

It's not top fill, he says, closing the book with the pen inside and sliding it back into its drawer.

She doesn't say anything.

All the environmental people signed off on it, he says. You saw, he says. They all signed off on it.

The collie dog heaves itself up off the rag rug again and he pets it.

Of course, she says. The government. Thank you so much for all your trouble. I just wanted to see what you had going.

He follows her to her car as if he doesn't trust her to get in.

Ten more trucks pull up at the gate and ten more trucks appear behind them. Their cloud of dust catches up, enveloping everything. A last vehicle, a minivan, drives around the line to where the kids have gathered. One of them coughs opening the car door, coughs hard. Even from this distance she can hear it.

The article was an inch long in the local paper yesterday, his daughter says, waving it at her father the minute he gets in. It appeared today—she waves another one in the other hand—

on page three of the *Herald,* with a headline: *Governor Not Doing His Job.*

He reviews each paper in silence.

You really got their attention. Wait a second—

She gets the phone. It's another one of her friends from her old job, offering advice. He can tell by her tone.

All through dinner she doesn't stop talking about what they should do next. I went to the dump and then called a few people to see if we have probable cause. We could file pretty fast.

Something should be done, I agree, he says, folding his napkin. You ever hunt? he asks her son, who's corralling his peas one at a time.

You'd take me hunting? asks the boy. He goes all aquiver with just the idea.

Dad, she says.

He'd probably be pretty good, he says, seeing that he spends most of his spare time shooting things on that machine.

Dad, she says again.

Her boy looks between them.

One of these days, her dad says, but he doesn't look the boy in the eye.

The governor calls not an hour later, the governor actually calls him, not the other way around. His secretary has to call twice because the old man says he can't hear so well, to try again. That way his daughter can pick up the extension.

The secretary stumbles over their last name, the governor calls him by his first.

My father, his daughter marvels.

I'm sorry I'm calling so late. It's off the record, says the governor. Thanks for your support at the caucus. I really appreciate it.

Of course, says her dad. He loves caucusing, he's about to ask about exactly when they're having the next one when the governor cuts to the chase.

About these trucks out in your neighborhood? I think you should let the Department of Environment Quality do what we pay them to do.

The news on TV says it's dirt that South Dakota doesn't want, says her father. What makes you want it?

The governor doesn't answer right away. Does he cover the phone with his hand? Does he turn to notes on his desk? Is someone signaling across his desk?

Frank, he says slowly so nothing he says can be mistaken, I'd like to suggest that you shut your mouth about this. In fact, I suggest you print a retraction.

Her father takes his own pause. I'll have to see about that, he says. Goodbye, he says.

I am not yet land-like, flattened, I am vertical is what his standing upright declares. He would announce this out loud if the boy was around but the boy is lingering for a haircut at his mother's behest. A boy his age needs to know about such things. In its horizontal way, the land crawls, shudders, slides, and a man has to stand up to it or else he'll slip under it. He himself has stood, and is still standing. He's a man who has raked the land with machines—no more wild anything—all his upright life, so much so he can actually feel the land's insistent tug: *Lie down.*

It's hot and almost every single cow is already lying down. He has to herd them with the pickup over to a feedlot full of silage. Dust from his vehicle swirls past where he's driven to inspect them, dust that settles around their sunbathing hides and his, the land never losing a chance to remind him it's waiting.

With the front of his vehicle, he nudges all the cattle to their feet. They're annoyed but malleable, they low and grunt and skitter out of the way, they follow each other into the dust, through the cloud of plastic and paper that's always hovering.

He wishes his daughter hadn't been on the extension. It was embarrassing. Now she wants to tell the whole world about the trucks, buy time on the radio and TV. Is he supposed to pay for that? She'd never make a politician. Real politicians work with compromise and she doesn't like that, she says it's lethal, all that dust. Nothing gets done without compromise, he tells her afterwards, not even marriage.

He shouldn't have said that, about the marriage. But the rest of it—if they talk about the dump too much, no matter how bad that dirt is, does she know that the bankers, who financed the land, might not lend him money for next year's cattle if they graze on the cornstalks? What about that?

A blackie sneaks away, over to the fence. He guns the truck in her direction until she runs back to the others, head high and sassy.

He's been a delegate to every convention since Goldwater, and owns a gold LP of Goldwater speeches to prove it. At the last convention in Philadelphia he wore red, white, and blue suspenders to hold up his overalls. He loves to cheer and drink and fill lots of rooms, small and big, with smoke. The party sends him off to every election because he's not as enmeshed in the chicanery of lawyers as those who practice full time yet he knows what's going on and can stand up for the farm people. He's acquainted with both sides—like Truman, he says, a comment that always makes the young ones roll their eyes.

He gets the gate. The cattle watch him ease it open.

Maybe his daughter moved all the way back here because she couldn't take the political heat. She said it was too many visits to where the environment had gone bad, and an office with windows you couldn't open, but maybe all these headaches and swollen joints of hers are just hoo-ha. After all, he's been around chemicals all his life, even the stuff those whining vets complain about from Vietnam. He feels fine.

He looks past the feedlot all the way to where the county road marker leans. Somebody will come down with a bad stomachache in a few years but that will be because his mother's casserole sat out too long, not from dirt troubling the water under the dump. At least that's how they'll spin it. He knows because he sat on the water board for a few years. Sediment cleans it on the way down anyway—it's like a charcoal filter. Although he's not so sure about these seventeen-syllable chemicals, how they work in that filter.

A prairie dog and three more pop out of the ground near the feedlot's trough. Noses alive, they perch not twenty feet away, opposite the cattle. There must be another hundred dogs in the making under his feet. Their holes catch the cows' legs and break them, and the mounds behind these holes are hell to plow around. Prairie dogs will ruin land until it's worthless.

Keeping an eye on the dogs, he shakes out ammo from a box of it under his seat. The dogs stand curious and friendly at the mouth of their holes. Some radio program said they face the sun in the morning with their hands folded, and again at night. They had better say their prayers. He takes aim at one, bracing himself against the truck door, squeezing slow, staring right at the first damn dog looking back.

He can never tell if he hits one because they all drop right into their holes when he shoots, not a one left to be seen, the land all horizon again, not a dog on the level.

He could shoot straight into the land.

Like peasants before a czar, the farmers approach the dais that bears the three DEQ employees, and Will who represents the dump. The corporation doesn't bother to send anyone higher up, not even after the governor decided to send in the DEQ with the facts. With their farm caps off and their heads bowed, all the farmers are allowed to do is comment on the facts, to give the community's land-experienced, tech-ignorant opinion of the impact of the dump on their property, and to ask quick questions.

She and her father take the front pew. She's made a lot of phone calls starting with *I am the daughter of*. The hearing's in what her father calls a meat-all-week church, not the Catholic fish-on-Fridays but Methodist or Congregationalist, churchgoers who rent out their sacristies for about anything. But today everyone comes dressed like it's church: he's wearing a Greek fisherman's hat instead of the ball caps of the other farmers, and a leather jacket. She's in her lady lawyer gear, black silk blouse, low heels, even lipstick. There's only thirty minutes of comment time. After all, it is a private corporation that has graciously agreed to discuss this, to make sure everyone knows what's going on—no one's up for a vote.

Will could be, grinning like a cat at the sound of a can opening. His part of the presentation shows the dump as a huge pyramid for investment—jobs, biomass production, even maybe an attraction as the tallest point anywhere near the Rockies. The DEQ nods while he speaks. When their science expert gets up to talk, he has inscrutable jargon on his side, studies that say such and such, words about a mile long.

The plan is she and her dad are going to bookend the comments, her first. She starts by asking why South Dakota didn't want to keep their dirt, as clean as they swear it is from a half century of bombs leaking into it.

South Dakota doesn't have a dump with special permission to store this type of contaminant. You do. The DEQ people talk fast all over again about how safe the dump here is for bombs. The dilution/solution, they say. We mixed it up real well with this plain dirt.

I'm certainly happy you didn't use any of the naturally radioactive soil of South Dakota to mix it with, she says. Even so, it only takes about one-thousandth of a percent of any of those munitions chemicals to kill us.

They ahem.

Did the fact that their governor was previously employed by the waste company have anything to do with how fast the permits were issued? she asks, she can't resist.

They say it's not a question they can answer. The reporter takes a note.

With her headache pounding from all the dry-cleaned suits in the room, she says, the aquifer flows north–south, right?

The expert nods, cautious now.

Most of the monitor wells are located well ahead of where the particulate would flow. Won't they miss any poison entirely?

I'm sorry, says one of the DEQ. We must give others a chance to state their questions. Next, he says.

The newspaper woman jumps up: What exactly is the effect on human beings if something ten percent more toxic gets into the water that everybody uses? That seven states under the aquifer use?

The head DEQ hands the newspaper woman a very thick book. Have a look, he says. Besides, he says, the plastic sheeting under the dump will protect you.

The Bishop men object, father and son, both so pigeon-toed they can hardly walk up to the dais. They say what they saw: ripped plastic sheeting. We called the boy who drove the bulldozer to come in today, but his folks told us he got a big bonus from Waste Management and went off to ag school early, says the son, disgusted.

All the farmers grumble, they look sharp at the Bishop men and back at Will who is reinserting some papers into a folder. Another farmer comes forward. The DEQ just caps the wells when the tests aren't good. Doesn't the water flow together? How can we know if they've gotten worse if you won't test the bad ones again?

We have requested the corporation to pay for repeat testing, says the DEQ.

Why would they repeat test when it might incriminate them? asks the newspaper woman.

It's not in our budget to do repeat testing, says the DEQ. They have to do it.

Those below the dais shake their heads.

Her father gets to his feet last, and clears his throat as if he's nervous. Is he nervous? His daughter finds that hard to believe—her dad, with the steely eyes, the no-smile-if-he-can-help-it? After all, the governor's afraid he'll talk. She was very impressed with that. Let him impress her again, let them have it.

He taps his nails against the dais railing. People don't fight enough out here to warrant another lawyer like him, he'd told her, but she thinks he prefers the quiet of the land to the squabbling. The land is what's important. He'll stand up for the land.

So what about the tipping fees? he says at last. The ones you earn every time a truck tips its load?

The head DEQ looks at his watch. We do earn tipping fees from the hauler on behalf of the state. Do you have another comment?

Her father shakes his head. His daughter shakes hers too, she's groggy and dizzy from whatever chemical they laid on thick to make their graphs, but she can't believe he's said so little. Where are the six killer points they rehearsed? What about all the dust blowing around, the disabled kids? She coughs. Maybe he's onto some new strategy and just hasn't told her. He's so crafty—he'll say he changed his mind, he'll make a last-minute dramatic announcement—

The DEQ calls an end to the meeting.

Okay.

Her father heads for the farmers going out the side door. She stands there stunned. Will and the DEQ expert are packing their papers. She wanders over, hoping to gather more information, a little sympathy, maybe even a little camaraderie, the way it used to happen after EPA hearings. The Bishop men don't shake her hand, they're disappointed too, but at least they're not wearing dry-cleaned suits. When Will winks at her, and she finds herself thrilled, flattered—and shamed, she changes her mind about hanging around the opposition. This time it's her father's property, someday her own water, not some client's. She backs off.

The newspaper woman sidles over and hands her the book the DEQ expert gave her during the presentation. What do you think?

She leafs through it to the munitions section and tries to concentrate on the difficult chemistry.

I'd like to give you more time with this, says the DEQ expert, snapping his briefcase open beside them. But the best I can do is send you a link to the report. He leans past the newspaper girl and takes the book away from her.

The psychology is clever: thirty minutes of spleen suggest they are heard, and two weeks later each of them receives a typed-up version of all of what was said, including their comments. All of the farmers like to see their names in print, he says, but most of them just file it.

Or burn it, she thinks, wasting the trees.

Around there, the cottonwoods grow fast, put down roots into the water table about the same distance down as the trees are tall. The dead ones bleach white and their bare trunks twist forty feet up in the air like it hurts to have to put in roots that deep. These white-trunked trees glow against the black clouds that scud up every season with lightning whirling inside them, ready to blow the trees apart. The farmers are as exposed as the cottonwoods. But they never feared the dirt.

Why didn't you go with the plan? she asks.

Her father drives through the corridor of cottonwoods, their leaves flipping in the rush of his truck. You could always live somewhere else, he says.

Not without a full-time job.

When he doesn't say anything, she says, I thought you needed a cook.

You're making me fat, he says, but she doesn't laugh.

She's sitting in front of the computer as if a solution to all that bad dirt will appear across its blank screen. Powered off, its blankness mirrors her mind. It's not the tingling from the shaving cream someone used in the next house sometime today—her sinuses aren't swollen. What is the problem, why can't she think?

Conflict: she has her fantasy, yes, father and daughter, arm-in-arm, briefcases on either side. He's probably teaching her self-reliance, how great it is to be on your own. She thought she'd learned that one quite a while ago. Doesn't he see that she isn't leaning on him, that he needs her now? It isn't just a case of protecting the world from bad dirt, he's old, his immune system is more susceptible to toxic chemicals.

She considers her son instead. A different blank screen. They'll have to move, the young have hormones raging that cling to any growth-stunting synthetic that wafts through the air. But first she will tell him everything she knows about the land and this dump, he has to remember about the poison, someone has to, or no one will know why the people here die. After all, it will be his land sooner or later. Sooner. She won't last as long as her father, that office job totally compromised her health. She'll have to figure out small lessons for him, a little at a time because he gets bored fast if she's not talking about something happening right in his face—or worse, he could get annoyed and hum while she talks, or stare out the window, letting her words drift away. He's that age.

The afternoon light shifts and she glimpses what across her face? A wet line from a tear reflecting off the blankness. Not sadness—frustration. Or anger bottled up, escaping. It makes her angry to see it, and she turns the computer on.

People are always making piles of paperwork until they look important, her father says two weeks later, slowly ripping open the envelope of his copy of the thick report.

Any mail for me? She tries to sound casual, crossing the kitchen to where he's standing.

Love letters or job offers?

She doesn't take that well.

No, he says, just your own copy. He hands her another envelope, then peers close at the pages in his hands. Why— look at that. They say right here everything is just fine.

Or course, she says, trying to keep her voice even.

Her boy, coming in behind him, hears her tone and gives her his *You mean me?* look. She frowns *no* as he secures a seat behind his computer.

I know fertilizer chemistry, pesticides, her father says.

True, she says. They're bad enough.

Bad? He laughs. What do you think keeps the crops in such good shape? He drops the report on the table. Remember when Will talked about biomass that the dump could make? I want to look into that. This dirt might be good for that.

Biomass costs a fortune to develop, says his daughter. She pages further into the document. There should be yellow and black tape around the whole area. There should be fences and suction pumps and moon suits for everyone. It should be cleaned up.

I suppose you're going to tell me I'd better not go barefoot, he says, taking a seat at the table and easing off his boots.

Yes, she says.

I'm old, he says. He pulls off his second boot. It doesn't matter to me what they put in it. Just ten percent worse than what we usually get.

She takes a deep breath. She knows going on about his immune system won't persuade him. But the farm.

He gets up to press a lever at the fridge until ice spews into his glass. You might bring down the value of the land talking too much about the dump, he says. That's all we have, land. He crosses the kitchen to pour himself a tall drink from the cupboard. I don't want people getting ideas.

Her boy prints something from his screen.

I've already got ideas, she says.

Her father stretches his arms wide as if in embrace, the drink gold at the end of one of them. You want to inherit, or what?

She doesn't know what to say. Is he threatening me? She says, It doesn't matter whether I get it or not—the land should not be ruined this way.

He shrugs.

She turns back to her cooking. The lyrics she grew up with went this way: *This land is your land, this land is my land, this land was made for you and me.* She pokes at something, she stirs hard. She listens to the ice cubes shift in his glass when he drinks. I'll lose both ways, she says at last. If I get the land, it will be bad and no one will want it, and I'll be sick to boot. Or I won't inherit any land.

The only way they'll stop the poison is if it runs in the streets of the capital. Come on, he says. He catches her hand and kisses it. You know you are the prettiest girl.

She isn't. She pulls away and walks over to the boy at his computer. What did you print?

He hands her the sheet.

Nice, she says and shows the sheet to her father. He has been listening, she says. Inspired, she says.

It's a buffalo with X's for eyes, its feet upturned, touching a pile of pink clouds.

It's just a picture, says the boy. I was trying out this new paint program. She pulls open a drawer and finds tape and sticks it to the fridge.

You're not the tattle-tale type, are you? asks his grandfather, sitting down at the boy's table.

He waits until his mother leans into the oven to shake his head *no*.

It's as if she hears which way he shakes. She whirls around with a hot dish in her hands. Leave him alone. All this time I've been trying to be like you—a lawyer, someone who stands up for the right side.

Her father gives her a steady look. It's only dust.

She sets the dish in front of him hard enough to break it. Yeah, but don't forget—dust thou shalt return. She plunges a spoon into the steaming food.

The boy has heard everything. His mother made sure of that. Then the boy forgets it all until the end of summer when he goes bike riding with a boy who is fast becoming his first new friend. He is telling him all about *the mountain*, what they call the dump now after all the truckloads have dumped so much more dirt in it, about how poison is dripping into all the underground water, that it comes from rockets and chemical bombs, how he heard cows dropped dead two seconds after drinking the water that seeped out from where they were trying to dilute it. When his friend hears about the cows dropping dead, he calls him on it.

Two seconds? he says. No way. He shakes his head.

The poison's out there. I heard all about it.

My mom reads the paper too, says his friend. She didn't say anything about it and believe me, she's safety first and all that. She killed the spider I had safe in a jar.

He shrugs. We could take our bikes out there and check it out.

You can't just see it, says his friend. But their talk moves on to experiments they've seen on TV with flames and bubbling liquid.

Biking out to the dump is no turn around the block, it's an expedition, pedaling a long way on a gravel road—well, the gravel's pretty much washed out since the last hard rain—but sometimes they can pedal with the wind so it's easier, and the sunflowers are tall enough this time of year they can ride in their shade from field to field, and the corn in between is almost as tall. His friend suggests they take along a plastic bag to bring samples back for experiments but he tells him about the thousands of plastic bags caught along his grandfather's fence line where the trash escapes the dump.

Really? Thousands?

They pedal long and hard, past big rows of sprinklers gushing out that prehistoric water his grandfather told him about, that his mother said it will take six thousand years to get back.

So is it historic now? asks his friend.

Before he can figure out an answer, they make it to the high fence that's tufted with so much plastic its barbed wire has disappeared.

That is a lot of bags, says his friend, leaning into the eight-foot chain link as if his body weight will make it give.

No guards here at least, he says.

A big swirl of dust blows toward both of them. They choke. The dust blows again, and another six bags get caught on the fence.

It's nothing, says his friend, peering through a break in the bags. Just a big hill. Not even any cows around. No puddles, pink or otherwise.

It's pretty mysterious, says the boy.

His friend takes another look and then stares at him. No, it's not—it's just dirt. He picks up one of the plastic bags and fills it with clods. I dare you to eat one, says his friend, offering. If you think it's so bad.

How hard can dirt be to eat? He's eaten burnt food before—Mom's mistakes. He's probably ate plenty of dirt when he was a baby. There's even a picture of him with a bug on his tongue when he was two.

I'm not stupid, he says, and he swallows a chunk.

His friend laughs hysterically, then pulls his shirt up around his face to protect himself from the dust, and bikes away.

He sticks out his dirty tongue when he catches up with him.

You were a liar from the beginning, says his friend. Poison dirt! You might as well believe in fairies.

He was going to say there are popsicles inside at his place, strawberry or orange, but the other boy pedals fast and turns his bike toward his own house at the stoplight.

He shoves open the kitchen door, and seals his face against his mother, who is wringing her hands. Where have you been? she says, it's getting dark.

He's surprised by his tears. There's nothing out there, he says. Nothing, nothing, nothing.

CORDLESS
IN THE FIFTIES

Past the pickled everything, especially the relish corn, past the pastry pies, their steam vents like eyes or pox with flesh showing through, past the stiff hem-stitched aprons flashing HOMEMADE because every seam shows perfect, past the pink and red ribbons on the sloppy first-aid kits, there—under the picture of the president—the door is open, left that way on account of the heat, slid clear into the barn side so the black beyond makes a wall where the bulb-light quits.

She can hear Harriet's pig whining out there for oat slop. It does that. The gelding has had oat slop every night of its existence, every night ten minutes after Mom said rosary, and today it has been sold to Safeway. They were supposed to pick up the pig or hit it over the head, whichever is more convenient for them, two hours ago, and Harriet has gone home to weep in advance. But the Safeway man has been drinking at the town barbecue—she watches out the open barn door—and has become so indisposed that he hasn't disposed of the pig, hanging around as he is with the rickrack queen, one of the Krasjewski girls whom nobody resists on a day off or on.

She won't tell Harriet. She will tell Harriet. She looks into the starry Ferris wheel turning fifty feet away, full of all the people she knows, and decides to tell her the pig screamed like hell the minute it got a good look at the Safeway man's mussed-up hair.

She can't go chase her down. She is supposed to see that no one walks off with the baked goods. The dry goods don't have a guard. She could take down and steal an apron or two but they are so ruffly and ugly she can't find the desire. The only thing she does want is a turn or two or four around that Ferris wheel and hopefully that will come when she gets her fair money, some fourteen dollars and forty-seven cents for some Early-To-Bed champion tomatoes she grew with special manure from Harriet's oat slop pig, minus the seed cost.

She is thinking how she should probably share the money with Harriet when a boy holding a phone receiver to his ear with no cord dragging crosses the open barn side. A car antenna pokes up on top of it, whipping the air over him. He nods to her and she pretends there is a lock on the barn that is stuck.

He passes by a second time and stops. I'm from the future, he says and hands her the receiver.

She doesn't laugh and she takes it. The why is because of his voice and eyes, eyes from that set of paintings she's seen in the carpet store, the ones with everything looking out of them, and the voice is the voice from a prayer book reader.

You ought to work here, she says, because of your voice. They could use someone like you on the Ferris wheel.

I know, he says, and points the jack end of the phone into the black. Talk.

She puts the receiver to her ear.

To be or not to be, she says, and giggles.

That's about right.

He walks over to the fence where so many wool jackets of the county's two marching bands are tossed over that the fence sags, and he speaks into his other phone himself.

When he comes back she says, Yes, she had heard him. Well, maybe she did.

I go to District Three, she says. District Three gives nobody the future.

I already got a patent on it. I've got two more patents, one for alarms that go off if someone touches a car and one for a sun cooker.

Wonderful, she says and she eases herself away from the door, away from the dark. The boy taps on his receiver, not noticing.

What else? she asks. She wants him to go on, to trip up so she can be sure he's not making fun of her. Others do, on occasion. But they are like the palsied jams marching in rows behind her: what you could count or hate only if you took an interest. She wants to like him, he's not the marching band.

I should renew the patents but that costs money, he says. My dad says wait until someone buys them, that you never put your own money into something to get it going. And now they're expiring.

You can get money winning ribbons, she says, but half of that dies in her mouth. She doesn't want to talk tomatoes.

But he hears well enough, like on a phone. Yeah? he says, stepping closer. Who puts up the money for the ribbons?

I don't know. She hates saying that, especially to someone who is so good with the future. A large slice of silence builds up between them, then somebody screams from the Ferris wheel.

I hear those wheels come off, he says. I hear they kill people. Now if you had one that went around like a saucer, he says.

The Safeway man is jangling his truck keys, crossing through the dark. It has to be him, nobody else would go to see pigs now. That pig of Harriet's agrees all at once, starts dithering like the Lord has called her personally. Only hers has a bell on its neck.

This is just a mock-up, he says, holding up his receiver. The real phone will be full of holes and flat—like talking to a piece of cheese.

Will he put his receiver down and stop touching his sweater placket? It is okay to be nervous, that is how she is, but the placket-picking increases with the pig noise. She is almost relieved when the pig goes suddenly quiet—oat slop?—she is almost happy to hear him ask: Do you believe me?

She doesn't answer fast so he will think she is thinking of the answer. Madras shorts is all she sees in her head, what you wear in the rain to get the colors to run. He has those on. Are they a new invention to get girls to look at boys there?

While she is not answering, he says: It doesn't matter, you'll remember me in the future, and he walks off, holding one receiver to his ear, the other under his arm, talking in such a voice.

He could have entered the phone in the Babysitter Aids Division or in Home Improvement and collected something. But she remembers that too late, when he has already walked to where the buses from the other towns are parked, and she can't leave where she is to tell him because staying is what she is supposed to do. She has to stay.

SALLY RIDES

I am inside the glass booth where no one can get in. Everyone can hear me, they tune in at two while I am cueing up and telling them about being tongue-tied with the time and the temperature, everyone in town tunes in. I mean, I go to school on Monday and the late lady tells me *asylum* is not *as-lum* the way the teletype suggested. But anyone who counts only listens to the songs. The school corridors are full of dedicatees, girls whose guys call in and I can usually make out what title their boyfriends want even if they're drunk. If it's for a birthday I ask, did you say bidet?

Like they know.

Sally, the queen of the corridor and more, homecoming twice, is adopted and Native American but nobody mentions that, they say how great she tans and what perfect flips she sprays into place, so thick and black, and what does she call her MG for fun? She is a cheerleader for herself and goes steady with someone new every week. The rings alone! I am inside the booth where nobody can bother me since it's Saturday when everybody else is off, when two guys, one after the other, request a song for her.

This happens a lot. She likes to do the four-way stop with the top down on her MG, waving to assorted hangers-on or examining her nails. Sometimes it is three guys. I mix up their requests but to no effect—the message in the songs is always the same: *Wow.* This time I have to play the same song twice. In between, I talk about how romantic the drive-in is these days, with its slushies and mosquitoes and bucket seats.

Like I know. I've never even driven past the drive-in with a male at the wheel.

I'm cueing up for the next half hour when there's a tap on my glass.

I spin around in my chair.

Some guy I don't know, old, at least thirty. Later I couldn't say what his T-shirt said or whether he had hair long enough to part. His hand was dirty, the one tapping the glass. A mechanic?

I don't even think *Who left the front door unlocked?* I have to get to the teletype in the next room in under a minute—I crack my door, I say, Can I help you? as if I'm some kind of carhop.

He pushes right past me. I thought you were blond. Your voice is blond. He turns that word into two syllables, the beer talking.

Excuse me, I say. I'm working.

He blocks the door. Fill 'er up, he says. That's what I do. Not really, he says, getting full blast my impatient look. I make cars jump, he says. He stretches his hands out as if sparks zipped between them. Not really, he says again.

I've got thirty seconds until news time. You'd better get out of my way.

La-di-dah, he says.

But he relents, steps to one side. I grab the headlines off the machine. It doesn't occur to me to run out of the station right then, although I do notice the back door's hanging open.

I get through the news with him standing right behind me. I'm best under pressure. A caller complains the ads are too long, I make all the right noises.

He's so still it's as if he's learning my moves.

Would you please leave, I say when I'm done. I'm having trouble, miscueing the long interview I grabbed—Robert Kennedy about something. Get out, I say, a little louder toward the machines I'm facing, and once again, swiveled around in my chair, to his middle.

He pulls out a knife. Bowie-style, the kind my brother got for Christmas that sits in his bedside drawer.

What's that for? I say. I can't look up, I'll expose my neck, I can't see his face, it will scare me.

Nothing, he says. Just cleaning my nails.

He cleans his nails.

For Chrissake, I say. I try to fix up the log and remember the ads I played but I can't, I'm too nervous. I search through the 45s for *Help!* by the Beatles but it's new and some idiot coworker must have taken it home.

You are about the most famous girl in town, he says.

I just talk, I say. I turn to the console, I press the Talk toggle On. I intro Kennedy.

The guy can't see the red on-air light over the door because he's too close to me, one nail left. I'll bet people call in requests all the time just to hear you, he says.

No, I say.

I did, he says. Twice, last week. You played them—*Lonely Boy* and *If You Could Read My Mind.*

Usually if nobody says who it's for they mean Sally. I don't even ask anymore.

Who's she? He squats down so I have to look at his face. It's empty. One pimple near the nose.

I toggle Off and then On, a sort of S. O. S. Could it be that nobody listens to Kennedy? She's cute, I say, and rich. You can see her about anytime in her MG cruising downtown.

He takes the phone off the hook.

Oh, I say, don't do that. I stand up.

The off-the-hook noise that usually goes on after a while is disabled for the station.

You seem pretty nice, he says, taking my seat, his knife still casual, still out. Can you sing? I imagine you singing or at least dancing while you work. He picks up the rubber chicken I throw at the manager when he wants country.

That's what happened to the last guy who came in here, I smartass to distract him, I step backwards.

Really? He drops it. Somebody else came in?

I shrug.

You're kidding me, right? There's nobody else but me who thought of it. I sat outside in my car a few times and watched the door until I figured they left it open.

He gets out of my chair and moves toward me. You let him in because you knew him. He points the knife at me but it's as if he doesn't realize he still has it in his hand. He moves it while he talks.

You're right, I say. The first part you said is right. I was kidding you.

Good, he says.

The interview reel is almost over. I catch it in place for several seconds while it whirls to a stop. Dead air. The reel cuts into my hand, it bleeds. I don't want him to get any ideas about blood, I put my hand behind my back.

Somebody comes through the outside door.

Before I can say how glad I am to see you, Sally sashays in. She's annoyed, really ticked off. Excuse me, she says to the guy, whose knife is gone, then she turns on me, hands on hips. You didn't answer when I called. And you've been playing dumb speeches.

This is her? he says.

I nod, punching in a commercial.

A smile runs across his whole face. He could be handsome but he doesn't need to be, he's older, girls in high school love that. Hi, he says.

She gives him her Hollywood best, every pearly white showing. You're from out of town, she says. It's a statement. She's dated everyone else.

I let the turntable start up an LP.

I'm surveying on the interstate, he says. Going to be quite a road, he says.

Your type, she snaps at me, and before he works that one out, Blinky shows up behind her. He probably had to park the MG. He wears contact lenses, is very big, defense, and recent. Who's the fag? he says. He calls every male he hasn't beaten up a fag. His friend Aaron comes in behind him, hulking in tandem.

The guys aren't happy, but not as annoyed as Sally.

Give Peace a Chance is what we wanted, she says, tapping her foot. Right away. They're fighting over me.

Just why would they do that? asks the guy, as if she's not the answer.

Aaron and Blinky get huffy.

Sally just now notices the blood dripping from my hand. Is that your problem?

Nothing, I say, I can't handle. Could you all please step outside and get to know each other better? You too, I say, with the flip of my hand to him. I have work to do.

The guy shakes his head. You're not a blond.

Ha, says Sally. That would take more than peroxide.

So great to see you, I say and I lock the door behind her and the three shoving, stalling suitors. After I dial the cops and run water over my wound, I run to the door window to see Sally still chatting up the guy leaning on her MG as if he's going to take it down his new highway, and the other two guys pawing at the ground for a takedown.

RODS

It wasn't the cowboy Rod who carried a football like an Xmas ham, who wore leather pants so tight the zipper placket showed, whose red curls I patted in my lap while I steered so innocently, so recklessly, onto a cloverleaf en route to college that two of the wheels careened as if in a cartoon. He sat up, his green eyes blue in alarm—I glanced—but said nothing. He always said nothing. Did I drive like that to make him talk? But even my show of car-abandon did not move him to express in words any fear or regret or true love or envy or even a single-syllabled *Why?* He did, however, peel my palm off the steering wheel and kiss it. Grateful he didn't die?

It wasn't Rod of cam + rod, with car insecurity, always changing make and model, his whatever car producing a roar outside the front door that could just as well be for my sister. He played trumpet in the cemetery with the window of that car rolled down, he had lip but not lips, we two agreed, he could mock put down every guy in the school and pun until I refused to say another word, he could talk but not kiss. He was protecting his lip for his instrument.

It wasn't the third Rod who was sweetheart-kinged and chose me to stand in his light, with flowers lassoed in ribbons in my arms as his date. Post-dance, he knocked off my glasses, asking What did I see? It was a straightforward exchange, he saw tit for tat and I had the tits. After a decent interval of *Ahem*, I asked if he had any particular feeling for me, since I was a mere sophomore telephoned out of the blue of status-seeking: my mother'd just built the town's first indoor swimming pool. Feeling? he said, his hands doing his best to provide an answer.

No, not that Rod. What I wanted was a Rod with real feeling, *Take that!* I wanted dramatic love with burning anger, the root of all danger, I wanted to feel feeling and know that I had fired its ignition. All boys my age wanted was to avoid being overwhelmed by girls. Cleavage and hips, the only trappings of sex they were certain of, dictated their clothing choices, their slouching angled to hide all arousal.

The Rod I ended up wanting came with a cheerleader whose father directed the marching band, and this Rod played guitar and sang with the cowboy Rod when he wasn't doing dishes to save money to buy his mother a new fridge. Blue-eyed like all the Rods, but his in slits in a face that showed too many freckles, he had a thickness of arms and legs that had made him a fat boy years earlier but now put him in uniform for every game. I caught him crying at his locker next to mine, alphabetical destiny. He rubbed his tears into his freckles and pretended to be giggling, then sly-eyed the girlfriend, the cheerleader not cheering our mumbled contretemps a hall's-length away. I took the look in his eyes to mean trapped, I patted him on the shoulder.

By midsummer, I had him grinding me into the sand long enough to be interrupted by another kid's dad, out night-fishing. This dark was punctuated only by *Gosh!* as Rod turned out to compete with cowboy Rod with his silence, making long gone cam + Rod seem almost attractive. Kiss-challenged or not, at least that Rod could talk. But there was no going back two Rods. Maybe the lyrics the Rods shouted during band practice channeled their every fix on emotion, maybe they didn't need to feel anything but the roilings of sex. Why had Rod cried? It had been weeks of me prattling and him goshing while silently tracing the top edge of my blouse with trembling fingers to find out his father was ill. Brushing sand off the lip of my bikini that night at the lake, climbing back into his car, I blurted out: What does he have?

I thought he was switching subjects when he yawned and yawned, I thought I'd plunged us into a thoroughly complete evening of silence.

No. It was more complicated after he spoke than before. He said he'd just made the last payment on the fridge, an avocado-colored one that his father had made fun of the day before. He said his dad hated him saving up to give it to his mom because that's what dads do. And he hates me because he's dying, he said, his voice breaking in the blue of the dark all around us, he said that his father butted his own head against the bedroom wall so he wouldn't cry out in pain, and all the night before he had heard this butting and that's why he was tired, not football practice.

There, I had it, a big viscous gob of feeling, as real—no, more real—than any adolescent *I love you* that I had for so long yearned to inspire. I had personally eased the feeling out of this flesh-and-blood boy in my arms, birthed it, as it were, and now he was really crying, sobless, wet-eyed, and mouth-twisted. I had no idea what to do—but he did. Could you leave me alone? he asked, he demanded.

I stood knee-high in the pricks of weeds beside the car, regretting the tone, if not the words I had used to extract this revelation. Between blows of his nose, with the crickets in the landscape serenading, a coyote somewhere beginning a howl at the moon, I started to fear Rod would drive away and leave me contrite and abandoned in the landscape, so embarrassed he seemed over his tears. I knocked at the door. When he opened it, the Grateful Dead were playing a tune on the radio that he knew on his guitar and he sang it: *It ain't no use to sit and wonder why, babe,* and air-guitared with one hand all the way home, filling the car and my ears with words, but not his.

It was shameful, the way I let him. Then, like a handoff in the third quarter of a quick football game, the next morning the cheerleader positioned herself next to my locker and took over. I didn't fight. His grief had overwhelmed me, I'd been touched. She must have known what to say, or how to listen better. Or maybe she never prodded or prompted him to evoke such sorrow. Six months later, post-graduation, post-cremation, he tuxedoed himself down the aisle with her. Six years later, he weighed three hundred pounds at the class reunion, with pictures of his children spread out before him, and her at his side, still trim and yoga-worthy. It was as if his emotions had solidified and hardened around him in shirt-stretching layers, or developed in the bath of the photos of the clones in front of him. He gave me a nod that could have been *yes*, you were right to have wrenched off my mask at that worst of all times and forced me to run into the arms of this woman and make the mistake of my life or Hi.

TWO FEET, FOUR FEET

If the snow is two feet falling, it is four feet drifting. The snow fills every dip in the county, it draws off what little holiday warmth there is and powders those hills that still hold brush and natural trees—those that the contractors haven't planted—and when the full moon makes every effort to search it out, the snow shows back black where it digs in deepest, where the truck founders, whines, and at last exits itself to charge their snowballs.

They fall back laughing with her dad's truck stopped short his mock ten feet away, so snowgeared-up they feel only the pillow of flakes under their down. That snow's white enough I could fix my typing with it, she says, coming over, taking a sip from the bottle her dad finds on the dash for the both of them.

Did you know that before four-wheel drive, kids pulled their own sleds up the hills, says her dad while they drop snow chunks onto his nice warm front seat.

That slick patch almost gave me a barbed wire lunch, says her boyfriend.

You're barely out of braces, her dad says.

She slides her hand around and under the boyfriend's parka to touch the skin of his behind, and leaves a handful of slush. Quit it, he says and brushes his bum to release it with only a squeal of complaint. She loses her mitten in this horsing around or so she says and they hunt for it on the floor while the truck makes its way up the hill, kissing twice dizzily, banging their heads together. They both sit up laughing, with their hands on their bruised skulls.

What's so funny? her dad asks but he's turned the polka channel up so loud he couldn't possibly hear an answer even if they made one. Twice the truck slips into a gopher hole or else just plain too much snow, causing the tree in back to ricochet around, but it's been roped in by her boyfriend who bought it for them. Her dad said he didn't want one but he didn't say no more than once. Its Christmassy shape comes from somebody in a cherry picker with a chainsaw, he told them. Now he works the gears and the pedal, and the truck finds purchase again. By the time it stops bucking the bumps and they crest to a flat place, she is saying, I will have such a long hot shower.

They all sit in the car, considering the view.

It can't be brighter out. The moon doesn't quit and you can see there isn't a single obstruction anywhere. You can even see where the train is coming from, that far, and whether a cloud has a chance if and when there ever is one.

Her dad lights a cigarette to the music or his shakiness and says, You don't need to go to college if you smoke, it makes you that much smarter all of a sudden.

I thought you thought college was a good idea, she says.

You have lots of good ideas, says her boyfriend.

I got in, she says. I can still go. She looks out the frosty window.

Her dad flicks ash and says, It is exhausting shifting gears, hauling the two of you up. The cost of the gas alone.

They laugh as if that's the funniest thing, and she says he should toboggan down with them. You used to, she says. Her boyfriend will even climb up the hill himself, on his hands and knees if he has to, and bring down the truck after.

All three of them have a nip. She coughs and sniffles.

Her dad says maybe.

Her boyfriend says it isn't getting any earlier.

The three of them assemble themselves tight to the toboggan, her dad in front. He wants to see what part of the morgue they are headed for. Tipsy, her boyfriend misses the back seat on the toboggan the first time, swerving and landing sitting up right next to them. This makes them laugh all the harder. Who pushes off? They sort of lunge into space, not onto the path the toboggan has taken before but high, through new snow. But the gravity isn't new. The speed forces a *Please* out of her that isn't about pleasure, then they slow as if they are touring the countryside on their behinds and come to a stop in a shush of snow that covers them all.

Her dad rolls off and throws his arms out flat. She stops screaming to swallow a big mouthful. Her boyfriend doesn't release her right away from between his knees, although she's spitting snow. All three of them gasp, while everything else is silent.

I'll whistle for the truck to fetch us, says her boyfriend. He rolls off the toboggan in a kind of slow motion that tangles her in a kiss her dad can't see.

I always know if I'm having real fun if I need a doctor, says her dad, brushing himself off. Get along now.

Her boyfriend doesn't stand around, he runs up the hill with big blundering steps, falling into the snow and out, and then out of sight.

She notices the cold after that, especially on her bare unmittened hand. Her dad stomps a few times and lights another cigarette and the smoke of it looks as cold as her breath. You never screamed so much when you were little, he says.

Now I know better, she says.

An animal calls from somewhere, not a pet sound, then the truck starts.

He's probably finished the bottle down to the last drop, she says, walking a line in the snow and back.

No, says her dad. I don't think so. He throws the red-tipped cigarette into a nearby drift and takes her bare hand into his pocket and holds it with his own glove off. They stand there with their shadows so close and so still they could be some kind of park statue. They hear the truck spin, then get high-centered, then her boyfriend drives it down.

I found your other mitten, he says as soon as he reaches them. He holds it out the rolled-down window. It dangles like a dead animal but she doesn't say that, then he holds it too high for her to reach.

They all get cozy enough inside, and her boyfriend starts fishtailing up the hill.

Something in her lost mitten smacks her knuckles when she puts it on and she cries out.

What's your bellyache now? says her dad. He is offering her the last swig her boyfriend has saved for them.

Just this, she says, and pulls a gob of ice from the wrist of her other mitten and applies it to her boyfriend's neck. .

He swerves for show but holds steady. Women, he says.

Her dad says they should take a break from all this horsing around and that he means it.

She is fingering the little box inside the mitten, one of the small kind that mean a lot of change is coming up fast and different from what she's planned. Just what do you mean by *women?* she says.

Her boyfriend steers the truck out of another ditch. I guess your mom was a woman.

Well, I guess she was, she says.

Flakes melt on her lashes in bunches, or else tears. Look, you made her cry, says her dad and she fake-laughs so hard it is as if even the snow is funny. You knew all about this, didn't you, Dad?

The old man nods, guilty as charged. He says, Let's go home put the tree up. You're cooking, right?

She says, Say please.

ENDANGERED SPECIES

This is the season? asks the older one with long pink nails.

This is the season, says the barkeep, slopping a rag between the two women.

You got my pocketbook wet, screeches the younger.

Well, take something out of it, says the barkeep.

I guess a little something will help, she says. She's blond here and there at the temples. But we're not that kind of women, she says.

You're in a bar, says the barkeep.

Okay, well, I guess a beer, she says, and squeezes her pocketbook as if the damp instead of money will be released.

The barkeep mumbles his beer brands but they aren't choosing. You pick, says the older, lighting a skinny cigar. So where is everybody?

The barkeep flexes a bicep at the mirror and says, You mean the men?

Both women laugh and look around the empty bar. You got it, says the older. Rich guys fly here to hunt, right?

The barkeep hoses two mugs full of the worst stuff and sets it down in front of them. A few. Who told you?

A friend. She also said we could stay with someone's mother.

Mrs. Darby, he says. Mrs. Darby doesn't put up with a lot of, you know, guests.

We want to get married, says the older.

What do you want to do that for? says the barkeep. Most of the women here want a divorce.

The older one exhales smoke. We have our reasons. Babies, for one.

That wouldn't seem so hard. He leans close when he says this.

Both women hug their purses and laugh.

A hunter swings in, huge, blood-soaked and happy. I got you some dates, says the barkeep.

I'll bet, he answers. Give me my lunch.

The barkeep brings out bologna and mayonnaise and white bread and starts putting them together. The hunter turns to the girls. Vacationing?

They shift on their stools. You might say that, says the older.

I have me two good dogs, he says back to the barkeep. Good for nothing but birds.

You look like you took the hide off something, says the barkeep. He lays the sandwich in front of him and divides it on the diagonal.

I got me a Bambi, he says, and bites at the bologna dangling from the bread. What do you two girls do for a living?

Receptionist, they say together. A big corporation, says the older.

They watch him eat as if he is starved. The younger one asks, What's there to do around here besides kill things?

We get take-out pizza, says the hunter. You got that in New Jersey?

New York, says one. Funny guy, says the other.

Not too many men where they come from, says the barkeep.

Not many straight men, says the younger.

Guys that laugh at your jokes? says the barkeep. He laughs. They're straight here, straight and narrow. Married, most of them.

I wouldn't say that, says the hunter. But pretty married. At least some of the wives think so.

Schoolchildren push through the fall blow outside the bar picture window, peering in now and then. You could try the high school, says the barkeep.

This is Winslow, isn't it? asks the older, stuffing her smokes back in her bag.

Winslow, Nebraska. Yeah, says the hunter. A mayo dab rides his cheek.

And this is the season?

If you mean hunting, it sure is. He puts his money on the bar and the barkeep takes it. Want to come watch me dress out? he asks the women. He pats his red-soaked front.

The ladies move their beers from the bar to a place at a booth. The barkeep raises his voice. She got the last one, your friend did.

The older one corkscrews in the booth to look at him. Look, we spent good money getting here. We changed planes twice and took a bus.

Sounds desperate, all right, says the hunter, looking through the toothpicks.

The barkeep puts the sandwich food back in the fridge behind him, then uncaps a beer for the hunter, who takes a long pull.

We can cook, says the younger one, touching the miniature jukebox jutting onto their table.

Me, too, laughs the hunter. I got a microwave and I get to waving it, believe me.

Gunshots ring outside the back door. The women jump.

Just a range set up with bales. The hunter holds down a belch. For the kids to practice on.

The two women nod and look away.

How'd you get here from the station? asks the barkeep, taking the mugs off their table.

Your town doesn't believe in cabs, says the younger. She kicks off a shoe and rubs her foot.

Taxi! Taxi! shouts the hunter, waving his arms toward the window. The last of the kids run off.

We tried Club Med last year, says the older. But all they have is families now, no singles.

Is that right? The hunter sways over to their booth, leans into it. His big hands take up half the Formica. You ever hear of Pole Creek Lodge?

That's it, that's it, squeals the older. That's where our friend said they were.

It's a secret kind of place, says the barkeep. Senators and the like fly in on government money.

So how do we get there? says the older. The younger starts to gather up her things.

The barkeep snorts.

I guess if I were in the market for a pheasant, I'd flush the undergrowth, says the hunter, moving off. I'm going that way.

We should've rented a car, says the younger.

The closest Hertz is four hours away, says the barkeep. On that bus, the one you just got off.

The two women toss their bags up into the truck's high cab, then help each other in. Hunks of what's in the truck bed in the rearview mirror shimmers in frozen pools.

The hunter turns off the radio after he eases them out of angle parking. Sixteen degrees above, it says. Below, with windchill.

Not so bad, says the older one, who turns up her collar. It's a dry cold, not from any ocean.

The town paving plays out in a minute, then the truck hits another kind of road and more things rattle in the chassis. The man turns and then turns again at a pump and keeps driving. The one with the long pink nails pops open her kit and takes out a file and smooths them.

What lines are you girls going to use on these poor defenseless senators? asks the hunter.

He thinks we have lines, says the younger, her hand out for her turn at the file. Men are all alike.

Wouldn't want the difference be just in the amount of money we make, says the hunter. He works over the wheel, steering the truck along at top speed. Where the road runs narrow, he stops. A rusted *No Trespassing* sign hangs on a gate.

I wonder if we should have dropped breadcrumbs, says the older.

A crew-cut expanse of gray-blond stubble starts a foot away from the sign. Over there, he says, pointing toward trees so far in the distance they look like fluff. That's where they are. Though I can't hear any shooting.

Can we get a little closer?

That wouldn't be fair. Not sporting. Besides, he says, those senators aren't going to be lying around the lodge on a day like today. They're going to be out doing what they paid for.

The two women climb out of the cab and shoulder their luggage. Are you sure it's them? asks the younger.

I'd suggest circling first, says the man, adjusting gears. Get them in your sights.

The truck sounds off as it leaves.

The older one thrusts her hands in her pockets.

I thought you liked the fresh air, says the younger.

If they marry you, you don't have to live here, says the older. They come from all over.

The frozen mud cuts at their pumps. They duck under the barbed wire, they walk. After a while, they hear an actual gunshot not so far away. I pulled the trigger on a gun once at camp, says the younger. I had a bruise on my shoulder for a month.

That's bad, says the older.

A bird falls out of the sky in front of them. It flaps and bleeds. They both back away as it gushes blood at their feet. They take more than one step back but are stopped by an orange-clad man with an actual gun who strides out of the brush.

You ought to be wearing what I'm wearing, he says.

Not my color, says the older, with new cheer in her voice.

The younger is trapped behind the twitching bird.

The man shoots it again and it stops moving. Can I help you ladies out? he says, picking the bird up by one wing, letting the blood jut away from his thighs. Where's your car?

We were just let off, says the older.

The man nods and jiggles the bird. Would you hold this for a minute? he says to the younger.

Sure, she says, not too excited, but she doesn't back off.

He tilts toward the sky and shoots something else.

The younger twists her face away from the bird bleeding so near her skirt. Do they have to be hunters?

The older one just smiles.

ALFALFA

The year I lick so much LSD off stamps I have to use Elmer's glue to back the twenty-center for a postcard affixed to a cash request to my mother, that *I am alive* note at the end of term, is the year of all the "wine" parties.

"Wine" is what we put down on a form to get the empty windowless room for the party, a room big enough to do a lot of licking and not see the walls pulse too close. People who are not throwing up from some real wine party or people fresh from not flunking or people who have taken to feeding and watering rats to get out of flunking, all my friends, when these people hear that Bugs will cook for a party, we buy a lot of these unlicked stamps, and even some wine.

That doesn't mean Bugs will turn up the flame and cook. He makes that clear. No pots at all, he says, all presentation. But as he has promised to do this meal for some time, and we have waited, party after party, begging him, we are really looking forward to it. I even find the jars he needs.

He already has a net.

Alfalfa rages beside the dorm, it is that much spring. Our building bisects the field, so many of us grad students with our new loans and our bad hay fever and our new-bought stamps with whatever drug on it to dissolve on our tongue tips, so many of us students here that they had to put up this concrete bunker of bunks and bare cells, of party rooms without windows abutting the alfalfa. All that alfalfa outside our bare cells keeps us in bed sneezing sometimes for days, it is that green, double green after a "wine" party.

The field is where he uses the net.

But first Bugs sends us off to the pet stores to buy every last chirper and writher, and we also pay a visit to the bait shop because people do fish here, and there are nymphs for bait. Then the "wine" boy says he has heard of a genetics lab down on College Terrace that Bugs maybe should check out. All you have to do to catch them is to shake them off the meat in the fridge. You want them before they get wings.

More and more of us sign up on the list taped up outside the party room, a list we keep there so maintenance will know we are serious and won't come in to check on where the smoke is coming from or if someone is carrying on a little loud. Pretty soon bets are laid on how much "wine" has to go down before anyone will stop licking and eat Bugs's feast. Such a bet is null and void for most of us. We will eat anything, we say, we will eat a lot of it, especially at this kind of party.

Bugs just shrugs.

We start the party an hour early, we who are already ravenous and lit, we start by spelling out Bugs's name in textbooks on the table. Or maybe just his initials. It is hard to tell, so many books keep falling off, and a lot of them mine, fresh from falling off elsewhere. The "wine" we finish fast then stand in front of the fridge to feel it take effect in comfort. It is so hot in that room with spring going on in the field outside and no windows to it that the fridge is the place to be. Two or three of us stand in front of it, flapping our T-shirt hems and bending to get our heads in a little, just in case there is something quick in there for the party, a Kool-Aid pitcher with a toothless grin, or toothpicks with flavor.

There is just the bait and the jars.

Bugs makes us back off and sit on the floor with our wild hunger in check. He unstacks paper plates and empties the jars and the bait with their bits and shows us how to pull off the legs and what to swallow whole. Some things he does cook, on a hot plate, but most we eat the way they come stuck to a little something like a cracker or a weenie. Some of us hesitate, yes we do, we harbor second thoughts, we turn our heads away and say, Maybe tomorrow. We sing then, apart and in unison, about an old woman who is going to die because of what she swallowed, then we drink some actual wine. We are all legal, all of the males over six foot but still growing, still a new size shoe every year but mostly sandals anyway, in snow or rain. We tend to hunger, even without a party, and we eat often, spread ketchup on napkins or chew frat key chains or stick the dog with forks and taste its kibble—if anybody is watching.

After a lot of stamps, we are known to climb trees after squirrels.

Bugs makes such a smacking noise eating, and raises his eyebrows with such a show of pleasure, that even the hesitant hungry are moved to try. He refills everyone's plates with what has been knocked off the bottles at the lab, small bits, and those have crunch, and there is quantity. He cleans these plates with the side of his hand and shakes off what clings to it while someone recites its families from the lab the way he remembers them while someone else checks the book with all those families that have not yet fallen off the table, that lies under a couple of those empty plates. The protein of the future, we say to the wriggling whatever, lifting whatever off the plate, and then Bugs makes up a few more plates and those we eat too, even with all the writhing and snatching and clutching at beards.

Some of us have beards then.

Bugs shakes his fingers through his, with long fingers that must've grown longer from searching around in the fridge or holding up this and that by the wing—his fingers are very long—he shakes those long fingers through the front of his beard that is already gray from all his grad schooling and asks, More?

More, we whoop as he offers them around. More is just about right, someone weeps. More, just a few, fall out from his beard.

The party is going, is gone.

The bloom is on the alfalfa that day though who would know it from the party room with its no windows that keeps us so safe from maintenance. More? Bugs asks one last time.

Due to our chorus, he gets out his net, whips it around the room in an S that ends over someone who claws at the webbing, and then leaves to avail himself of the bloom.

We keep on "pouring" refreshments, such as they are, and talking up species and flavors and the crunch of it all until he gets back, sweaty, with the fat net knotted tight. A bit of bouquet on it, he says with a chuckle, and fits all its furled green buzzy insides into a bowl just the size for a salad.

Chilled, he says. You'll like it better.

We play music, we play who can see the spiders that some of us can already, climbing the inside walls looking for a window, big spiders the size of the fridge with hair on them and green eyes and poison flowing from their four mouths. Then we play *Who is hungry still?*

We get to punching the fridge.

Bugs says Enough. Enough with the chill. He puts the bowl on the floor and skinnies the net's insides into it. Shshshsh, he says. From under the green alfalfa stirs the rest of our meal. It stirs and chirrups and clicks like safes opening in old movies we have just seen for the first time in black and white or like a brush across a drum someone is bringing out now, is brushing, is now pounding, it stirs because the night is warm and the fridge is cold and what are these insects doing there on the table and not out in the field, alighting and alerting each other?

We eat them all, scrabbling through the bright green for the brushing and the stirring and just as often eating the alfalfa stink that gets stuck to a bug or gets in the way of someone else getting to what we want. A kind of explosive eating breaks out around the last elusive bits and just as these bits are getting eaten, Bugs plucks, with two of his long, long fingers, at red ones trying to fly off. Then he sings about flying away, the house on fire, and how he will help the ladybug.

Her, he says.

In the end he catches six of them right out of the air. Later, of course, it is ten. He chews every one of them straight down while we cheer, then he closes his eyes and gives off some gas from deep from inside himself, something his body has made in a hurry. They could have pesticided that batch, he tells us.

You can already hear the flushing. Many partygoers don't make it, they just sit in corners on the floor, staring at their hands where whatever it is comes up with the green, and Bugs too, with the alfalfa the secret ingredient he regrets swallowing, now moving through all his personal passages.

The next day there is a rush at the cafeteria for potatoes mashed to a paste, for eggplant peeled of batter, for clear Jell-O with peaches. We eye all that is concealed in the sandwiches, we strain soup for what floats. Some of us swear off all meat, not just chicken, what everything you don't know tastes like now and forever, but our future is already growling in our stomachs, and none can deny for the rest of his life: I ate it.

AFRICA

A deer came right through the windshield, her father says, and taps the stretch of glass in front of him. Came right through, and knocked the guy into the backseat.

The deer was dead on impact?

Come on, he chuckles, pushing the car lighter in. What saved the guy was not wearing a seatbelt. First thing, the car ran up onto the train tracks.

Of course a train was coming.

Somebody going the other way stopped and dragged him off just in time. If he'd had that seatbelt on, he would have been pinned inside.

His seatbelt swings limply against the car wall where it has been jerked from its buzzer. I rest my case, she says. I'll watch for deer instead.

He laughs and lights his cigar.

What do they call those small white birds that sit on the backs of the cows? she asks.

Ibis, he says, between puffs. Just like in Africa.

She pulls idly at her own broken seatbelt. I knew that, she says.

He drives past a windmill, the single perpendicular in any direction, its blades chopping the air in blurred circles. From inside the car, no other sign of wind is evident across the empty prairie except for the car's shuddering on the county correction curves. Look at those pretty polka dot horses, he says, by way of staying awake.

That's what they call pinto, right? she says.

Appaloosa. Pinto's for beans. Those are pinto. He sticks his free arm toward the scraggly rows that fight the brush. Some days I like growing beans better than judging. Judging gives me a stomachache.

In Sudan, she says, all the cases come to you—or else you get borne on a litter to the next one.

What a good idea—the weight of justice on the plaintiff's neck. He knocks ash off his cigar. That sure would shorten up a case or two.

A small town reveals itself a mile off, signaled by a stretch of fence posts covered, each one, by a cowboy boot. He slows when they come to the town's single intersection, turns down its one paved street and parks in front of an old schoolhouse marked *Café*.

This is what education's come to, he says. Or else they turn the schools into junk stores full of antiques—this one's antique food.

When they enter, the prosecuting attorney lifts his coffee spoon toward them from the first booth. You're late, he says, with a smile that looks easy.

If I'm early, I have to pay the check, he says. My daughter, the one out of Africa.

Welcome back, says the attorney, shaking hands. Not much of a tan.

It's been ten years, she says.

A person gets marked, says her father. She's a marked woman.

Dad, she says. That's right out of the movies.

A masculine blond swings out two plastic-coated menus by way of a greeting and herds them into the booth. The three of them turn their faces up to her when she pulls a green guest check out of her waistband. Nothing special today, she says.

They order nothing special and the waitress writes nothing down.

The attorney sighs into his coffee cup. Did you know, my dear, that right here is the richest town per capita outside of Saudi Arabia? I mean it—with the cattle market the way it is. And they can't even put together a decent lunch. Probably just like in Africa.

It wasn't hard to order lunch in Sudan, she says. You ate what there was.

The attorney looks at her father. She sure is one of yours.

She's not around much anymore. I blame that on her trip. He smiles and pulls napkins out of the container. So who's done what to whom this week? What happened to the harassment?

Out of court. They moved in with each other.

Ah, crime, her father says, rubbing his hands across the napkins. She files a complaint every time she's in season.

As regular as a bear, says the attorney. Pardon me, he says to her.

We're out of vegetables, interrupts the waitress, unloading her forearm of plates. How about crackers as a substitute? She offers sealed Saltines.

With pickle relish? says her father. That'll qualify.

She leaves six packets of crackers and one of relish and they eat slabs of meat and mounds of starch while the attorney picks his teeth. I heard about you, he says. You worried your father.

Not Dad, the guy who won't wear a seatbelt.

That's just another thing those car people make you pay for. You know his problem? The attorney points his toothpick at her father's forehead. He's got imagination. He's a soft-hearted bastard who gets bad dreams. Am I right, or what?

Her father pats the ketchup off his face. I'm just a farmer with opinions. That's why they elected me.

Right. The attorney leans forward. Just one of the best lawyers in this part of the country. When are you going to stick this judging business and get back to some real law?

That's laying it on a little thick. Her father waves at the waitress and points at his cup.

The coffee's actually good, says the attorney.

The waitress pours three lukewarm cups, then, with great flourish, signs her name to the bottom of the practically blank check and places it on the table.

The attorney picks it up.

What? Paying for poison? Her father laughs. That's what I call influencing the judge. He slaps the attorney on the shoulder and takes the check away.

They file out of the café onto the half-buried cracked sidewalk and blink into the sun. So that was fine. Her father moves his belt a notch and re-tucks his pants. See you next week.

Oh, there's just one little thing. The attorney finds a document he's stuck in the folds of his newspaper. They're in jail now if you want to have a talk with them.

Her father glances at the paper, and then again, rubbing his eyes behind his glasses. A dog case? You need an autopsy for a dog case?

Hey, says the attorney. It could've died in Kellen County and turn out to be somebody else's problem entirely.

With the attorney following them, they drive the three blocks to the county jail. How's your digestion? she asks.

Guilty, he says. He turns the car onto the upgrade next to the sheriff's car. Three young men loiter under a tree in front.

Just look at the silver on that one, she says. It's a wonder they can stand upright.

Rodeo awards, says her father. They make the buckles bigger every year.

They're friends of the accused, says the attorney, coming around to the jail door. There's a cow meet this afternoon and we've got the best wranglers inside.

You do have a little something, says her father.

Oh, boy, says the attorney, holding the door open for them.

The sheriff is asleep at his desk as if he's being paid to do it. They don't bother him, they walk through a door marked *Open* where a bare light bulb dangles overhead and two chairs meet a table. Just look at this, says the attorney.

A county section map is tacked to the wall behind him. Pinned to it is a cutout of a collie. Red string radiates from its belly fur in a crazy crisscross. Here's the gas station, he says, pointing to a green-headed pin. And here's where we found the body. He presses a black-headed pin a foot away.

You just don't have enough to fuss around with here, do you? says her father.

Well, says the attorney, yes.

That sure is a long way for a tail to keep burning, her father says, tracing the string.

They put the nozzle into her and gassed her up.

The attorney fiddles with a chair back. After she caught, she tried to bite her rear end. The way they do.

Her father ducks his head as if avoiding the cruelty. You don't have to stick around here if you don't want to, he says to her.

She shakes her head.

He turns back to the attorney. So, who do you want me to talk to?

Actually, the parents. They just want to leave some money and have the whole thing dismissed. They can pay, believe me.

That's letting them off pretty easy, says her father, taking a Tums. The punishment should fit the crime I think. Like they do in Africa.

I don't know, she says. An eye for an eye?

Punishment? The attorney looks nervous. They'll fight it.

Her father looks disgusted as if the attorney himself did the job on the dog. Let them go to the Supreme Court for all I care. Big deal. First off, collect the bail. You can make that big. Then they'll get to half-strangle calves in the rodeo and be happy. I'll come back in a week when it cools down a little and try them.

If you say so, says the attorney.

Her father looks out the window at the rodeo contestants. And remember, this isn't settled out of court like your bear woman. This is the State vs. a bunch of mean rich kids.

The attorney fools with his tie clip. I'll tell them.

They drive to the next courthouse where at least there's a Dairy Queen. They drink malts, leaning up against the hot car. I'll have each of them tied to a dog for a week, day and night, her father says. The first I hear of any abuse, they'll really pay.

Ah, civilization, she says.

He's fumbling around for a new cigar. You know, he says, my stomach feels better now that I've decided on a sentence. Maybe I could get used to this judging.

In Sudan where I went, if the judge turned out to be wrong, he had to serve the sentence.

He raises his eyebrows as if he doesn't have to believe her. Why did I waste all that worry on you?

You never worry, she says, her straw making noise at the bottom of the cup.

He lit his cigar. Maybe. He looked at her over his puffing. But maybe I drive a little slower when I have you around.

ALL MAPPED OUT

Best not to think about talking, best just walk straight in and get through to the *Sorry*. Why, this is the very same room he walked through on his way to see his son for the very first time twenty-one years ago, changed now from Delivery room to Reception. A nurse waves a clipboard at him in a spanking motion toward the next door.

The air feels thick around this door where he presses it. He knows what's coming, he doesn't want it, god, he doesn't want it, he has to walk another step and there, behind the door—

Her hands dangle at her sides, with some kind of apron thing around her waist with ties that dangle too, something you'd never wear outside a kitchen. He finds a place in front of the TV some idiot has left on and says to her, Sorry, our family is so sorry.

She nods at him. OK, she says.

He waits for something else. She cups her hands around the front of her face and her shoulders shake. A man holding a pair of boots—the boy's?—tries to quiet those shoulders without putting the boots down.

He backs out saying, Sorry.

His wife is there in the hall finally, cell phone silent. Seeing her enrages him, left as he was to say Sorry alone. He hisses, You too—go on.

The way her eyes wander he can't tell if she's heard him. He points.

Don't you want to know how your own son's doing? She shakes a crushed hankie between them. He could be worse.

Scratches is what the cops said.

That's not true, she says. The trauma alone.

His lawyer brother draws a map on an old gas receipt. Here is the intersection, here is the sun, coming up too bright, and the boy was just going a little too fast, he says. He points at the skid marks with the golf pencil he has found in the seat folds.

He was loaded, he says.

But the sign is half covered in mud, says his brother. He waves the shred of paper over the truck's hood. Or it could be, if nobody took a picture of it. And here—he made the skid marks, they didn't.

He snorts. I don't want none of your legal aid.

I could get him off, his brother says. Or get it reduced. It was early—misty—I heard the weather report. He rubs his face. Nobody was really speeding.

Mist, he says. He stares at a set of car tracks that veer off. I don't know what to tell you. It was nine in the morning after his graduation party and he was drinking.

This is when he cries.

With farmland here, grid is all. You've got your right angles and your circle irrigators and some cover, but even in the summer the cover is never higher than a coyote, it's not like you drive up to a corner and there's a tree blocking your view. The aerial map shows the grid, bone-white against gray, and a lot of written-on numbers for whose land is whose. Nothing in the way of a view, you can see everything.

His son lies in his old room with just a few bandages sticking to him, the peel-off kind, but his father keeps coming in to tell him what? How big can he make that *Sorry*? Basketball-sized, something you couldn't just hand off or hide—bigger. His son pretends to be asleep. Then his son sits in the game room in front of the tube and sometimes even changes channels, he gets so interested. You are going to do time, his father says, and the boy doesn't even blink. But he doesn't go back to his apartment either. Once his father catches the smell of alcohol on him but his wife says it's the rubbing kind in case of infection. He can hardly blame him for wanting to drink. A whole day's worth of basketball or Little Johnny soap operas can't solve his problem. But when he finds him passed out on the sofa, he pushes him off hard.

He never spanked him.

His wife thinks they should move. She doesn't get it that they can't move. He is still trying to figure out a way to go forward on the land they have now, let alone move. He can't just go into some town and get a job at a filling station. If the judge asks him to testify at the hearing, all he can say is Sorry, we're all so sorry, all over again, and the law will find his boy guilty anyway, sorrow or not. Other people—he knows this from TV, on a show he watched while his son vomited out of nervousness or stayed in his room—other people give cows or money or even guns to the aggrieved family and call it even, or say they do until somebody pops off somebody else from the other side a year later.

In no way will his son be enough for them, slug that he is now. He knows it will take himself to even up, he knows that because that's what he would want if somebody killed his son. I want the guy who put him on Earth.

He is lucky the boy had no father. The man with the boots was a boyfriend. Boyfriends are different in that they are just in it for the fun. He is also lucky they have no money. Not only because they can't hire somebody to kill him—that isn't so far-fetched, a guy did that a couple of years ago in the next county over a wrecked Subaru—but because they can't hire a hotshot lawyer and take everything from him in some civil suit, just the way those families with their cows do it.

He has a few cows.

He's standing out on the southwest section of the West 40 near the Tickle ranch. He's thinking of course of selling it just the way his wife wants, and going somewhere where the grocery baggers will look him in the eye and the priest say hello. It is not two weeks after the hearing. The paper showed his son hiding his face like some badass hip-hop singer leaving the courthouse—and he thought the editor was a friend! But the wheat has come up anyway, his son having sown a section just before the accident. He did a pretty good job of it for a college graduate. The plants pick up a little shorter where he finished the row for him, where snow had fallen into the scraggly green shoots.

Every night he pushes open that door.

The boy will make license plates for twenty-two years, in bad company. Oh, his uncle will get him out in five and he will marry someone eventually, not that Hardy girl who had her heart set on him, no, but sex will goad some girl along, and then he will not drink in his home or he will, because of all the life of his that has been left off.

He drives the pickup down the road slow. He drives slow because there isn't any hurry anymore, about him or his son, or them together.

They want him? They have him.

MENNONITE FOREST

Released from the pickup, I'm instantly snow-ankled but I'm also down-coated and piqued, that is to say, doggone in wonder at the stand of ratty Chinese elm let grow at the edge of the circle, a circle here being the swath of a sprinkler system pivoting itself around a wheat field, and my father being the last one to let any inch of land go to pot.

Go on, take a look, he says.

I enter the forest. This part of the world being underrepresented in forests, this part of the world barely supporting its trees and those being mostly bare-assed cottonwoods, it is a vision, this forest of elm. Not that the Chinese elm is much more than trash, water-sucker trash. But Dad hates trees so the appearance of a stand on his actual property, a guy who axes the slightest growth of vegetation if it doesn't bear grain, makes it worthy of inspection.

We have just come from a lilac farm. He had to make that place sound like the plants were milked or fed or at least a real crop so as to be acceptable to his shunning of trees, and we did agree that it couldn't be called a lilac ranch. There was no herding involved. Rows of every lilac variety and color show-pieced the place, plants ten feet tall and in bud, if not bloom.

We stood on clumps of plowed dirt between the rows and sniffed and warded off bees in the snow.

I want to say there was a reason for this stop at the lilacs, to commemorate this or that or even to buy a plant but similar to the stop at the elms, we were just in exit, meandering home, to his, not mine. I'm usually three thousand miles off, here just to keep house for Dad for two weeks.

Drive closer to the lilac farmer's house, he said once we were finished with sniffing, and keep your eyes peeled for the baby grand inside. I wheeled us up short to a formidable pink bush in the front yard. The house will never sell, he said. A place with a front room and a piano like that?

He rolled up his window on the snowy spring air, with the bees falling to the ground, having caught too much snow on their wings. Some people like music, I said. He shook his head, skeptical, while I maneuvered back out onto the gravel and down the road.

There's where the Mennonites turned out that fellow. He pointed opposite the piano-cursed property.

When I drove past, the house was no plainer than any other: flat ranch, driveway, front door, only a little more rundown than the house we left behind, with its piano room. Turned out why?

Dad was fooling with the heater. Right up to that front door walked a twenty-five-year-old man, he said. A twenty-five-year-old man. He shook his head at the number. The twenty-five-year-old knocked on the door and when the man answered, they both nearly had a heart attack.

Sounds like a fairy tale, I said, stopped at a sign, wondering which way to go.

It was. They looked exactly alike. No DNA test necessary. The man had to leave his wife and kids and move away.

I guess Mennonites aren't big on forgiveness.

Dad scumbled the inside of the windshield with the chuff of his hand to get rid of the haze we were making, breathing. Let me take you somewhere. Turn right.

We drove to this circle corner I am walking into now, with its forested bit. The Mennonites use it, was all he had time to tell me before a corn-planting, fertilizer-bearing friend came up out of the dusty snow in his pickup to talk.

The first trees of the forest, when I reach them, are only about seven feet up, leafless, strewn around an entry path I take, not touching their budded snowed-on bare branches lest they seem more real. The snow is pretty much skim milk against the rest of the trees, with blue between bands of gray-white where a mysterious dust has thrown itself against the melt.

I come to a clearing. More blue shines from between the spidery branches that encircle an actual arbor made of elms twisted into a support, a place you could marry or commit bloody sacrifice. I turn around to face the pinkest of sunsets. The flat bare pink plain is stained for miles.

Did you like it?

I'm back in the truck. Dad has honked and I have high-tailed it before he can leave me as he is wont to do, with high impatience at the accelerator, conveniently forgetting he's too old to drive.

Spooky, I say along with my nod.

I let the trees go all these summers I rented to them—thirty so far. The little Mennonite kids always get a kick out of it. He switches to four-wheel drive for the new mud that has formed under his wheels while he chatted, and he ignores my offer to take the wheel. They don't have computers and basketball to play with, he says. They don't have a father. Or they didn't after that fellow left. But before then—well, there weren't many places to meet a woman.

You're a surprise, I say. I eat a yogurt, practically frozen, wedged so close to the door. Dinner will be late because I'm cooking it, Mom being no longer interested in the job. I look into the glaring sunset we drive into, toward home, thinking of the trysts in the young Chinese elm forest that Dad is responsible for or even his own, and of the shunned man driving away from his family with his new son into the sunset of his life, and last, of how romantic he is, my old father, with his lilacs and forests and no one but me to forgive him.

MUGSY

Mugsy wasn't his name but it should have been. He wore a porkpie hat, according to Dad, who has trouble remembering what they are called—the name's a dish, he says. Dad's looking out at the snowy rows of sheared wheat that's making up what scenery he's not slept through, and telling me about Mugsy's case. An overpass reminds him, and like the telling of any tale, several overpasses pass before Mugsy is a fish that can swim—Dad's way of saying when all the pieces start adhering, story-wise.

The porkpie hat Mugsy set way back on his head the way those Jews do. It looked like a kind of halo, if a halo had black felt and Jews wore them, Dad says. Mugsy didn't take it off coming into the courtroom so the sheriff had to show him how to do his duty. He probably never removed it, not even at night or for a bath—this was before showers got to be what everyone took. He stank—the whole courtroom covered their noses—all five foot and maybe five of him. But he liked the ladies and wore some of that toilet water. It was one of them who turned him in.

Dad really enjoyed being a prosecutor so long ago. It meant he met people who just went ahead and made mistakes or people who didn't see the world as a problem, especially with regard to ownership.

Mugsy cracked safes, he says. You could see he grew into it, even in his build, the shortness in his legs and his hammy arms. He looked as if you could twirl a combination lock on his chest and he would yield gold bullion right from inside himself. The arms were for getting the rest of him around a safe and lifting it. The small banks around here—Dad points toward the end of a snowy row where nothing ever so bank-like as even a gas station interrupts the view, points as if small is a distance—the banks here didn't have as much money in them then, most money sat in the back of the lumberyard or in the hardware store in a register. Not like it is now, with people running to a teller twice a day to make deposits. Businesses had safes on the premises that they emptied the register into. Mugsy specialized in that business-sized safe, not only because he could hug one right onto the back of his pickup but because he wasn't much good in the safecracking department.

Me, the driver, the straight man, I ask: So how did he get them open?

Dad optimizes the suspense by blowing his nose. We have just come from the track. The horses here run even in a snow-storm but just looking at a horse through the glass of the box makes Dad sneezy. I'm driving because he sneezes so often, and because when he makes his points, he has to turn completely to one side to watch my lips for my answer, and doing so, he has slid the truck into the snowy bumpy part along the side of the road, aka a bank, where we switched drivers. But it was the overpass we drove under that reminded him of Mugsy.

He'd transport the safes in a truck to an overpass, wait until all clear—no cars coming—and throw them down one at a time to open them.

He must've had a partner to collect the flying bills at the bottom. I imagined the freefall, the ecstatic anyone coming upon the scene.

Bills come in bags, says Dad. Mugsy said once his shirt tore off when a safe handle caught on it and he almost lost more than his shirt.

You'd never know beforehand if it were worth the trouble, I say.

It was a better bet than those horses.

What would Mugsy have done today at the track? I ask. Put a firecracker under Five?

Dad is asleep just like that but he has told me to keep him up, that he doesn't get so many chances to chat. Did they ever get his partner? I ask as loud as I can, and still sound cordial.

Dad's face snaps awake. It was probably his wife. We didn't prosecute a wife then. She had the kids. When I asked him why he stole all those safes, he said the milkman needed the money.

You remember those very words?

That and the hat—what did you call it?

A porkpie.

A lunch hat. Dad stares out the window while a snowy town dismembers itself alongside the highway: car parts, billboards, *slow* signs, implement stores.

I'll bet more on the horses next time, I say.

Thatta girl, laughs Dad. Don't be afraid to break the bank. The milkman can wait.

And he is asleep again, head to chest. I think. He turns to me with his eyes still closed. We caught him that time with a broken safe. It was empty.

That means some overpass might have a bag of bills hidden nearby from forty years ago.

You put it like that—yes. He scans the highway, blinking. Still a better bet than Five.

Five was a gray horse. Nobody bets on the grays, I say.

Your mother liked gray.

She's not dead yet.

I'm not a betting man.

The town breaks around us but we don't stop. She hates me, I say in somebody else's voice.

Dad says nothing. What he hates are complainers, the world is full of them. Be different is what he likes saying. He's still saying nothing. Maybe his hearing apparatus has shorted.

I glance over, then put my eyes back on the highway. He's making some sound, but not words. I can't tell with his glasses whether he is feigning noisy sleep, or sobbing.

I drive on, overpass after overpass, looking for bills.

PRAIRIE DOGS

We shop like days of yore, until all the fabrics and styles we pick out appear in piles at the register. When we were left at home as children, our mother did this same kind of wild shopping and had boxes of merchandise sent back, with tissue in the corners and deep in the sleeves. The trying on of it all tried us, we girls fought for and fit so many of the same. Now none of us try anything on, it's all for her and easy to fit with her shrinkage: we choose just the smallest in wild colors her skin complements even now.

Her three-hour morning makeup is complete she tells us by phone, so we can knock without fear on her door of Extended Stay, the one with the unforked or -spooned dinner outside it. She makes it to the door, skips all words of greeting because she can't find the knob exactly, she can't quite think because she's been drinking with all her making up, and still shrinking, her food so untouched.

She is always late for him. Even here, in her new suit and shoes, even now, with his operation imminent, she minces forward not too fast, down overlit corridors toward the room where we discover he is no longer. The nurses laugh—they do this automatically, often—they say he was gurneyed away long ago. Patients do better when they have relatives, blames one of the nurses, the success rate rises. We don't take that kind of comment so well, what with the late mother looking for her new drink, and the doctor not out golfing but cutting or roto-rooting into him already.

The doctor we see after the operation has no face except corporate. Where one cuts, he says, as if someone else held the knife. Whose blood is he afraid of? we ask each other but not him. Others are scheduled for him to work over, others have wives waiting just as dressed up but punctual.

But not as thirsty. We won't fetch her flask from the glove-box, we won't, and she can't walk that far. Not that she asks, she leans way out in her seat and says, Who isn't so busy?

We are all equally busy, one doing his taxes, one crying wolf with her daughter so she can go home, one dialing and dialing whoever will answer, one eating a lump of a leftover taken in haste from three hundred miles away, one wringing his hands until eczema flies.

Social services, says one to the other. We could have them help us.

Social services says *no* so obliquely, in referrals, in *Call someone else,* then just No in the face of all of us, while she flasks somehow in the bathroom. She'll kill him with the stress of her drinking, we say, isn't that social enough? What about the service?

Then he is finished, and then he isn't, he's pulled back in for another something, he's shower-capped again and green-suited, resprayed with antiseptic that looks like rusty blood. We just get a minute to show how we shopped, we show him her all dressed up.

My pussycat, he says.

After he's taken away, the eldest one says, You'll kill him, to her face but she, in her new bright clothes, just laughs. Me?

We stare out the window. It shows a prairie dog town, not one planted to amuse us in a zoo but wild, with a dog waiting in front of each hole. Bubonic plague says one of them, that's what they have. I read about it in a magazine.

I'll run in and pet them, says another.

Then he emerges a second time. While he's reeling in consciousness, the designated doctor allows us the pleasure of watching the video version of his performance. It's beautiful, all that ragged symmetry, his timely chopping and sewing though who knows, one of us says, whether it isn't the airline copy, the same show for everyone. Fasten your seatbelts, says the youngest after we're dismissed.

Get the doctor to talk to her, chorus the others, thinking to waylay him. The doctor will confront her with his degrees and his years of service and the weight of health insurance and liability, not to mention malpractice. We have to find the doctor again and ask him to, with our timid generalities and helplessness and handwringing. Over time things change, says the doctor once he's cornered, instead of reproving her.

Is there social malpractice? asks one of us, walking away.

Back at the waiting room, she complains the hotel smells, why isn't he finished?

He's finished, we tell her but she won't go see him. We offer our interest instead, we converse while the youngest takes the car and goes shopping again for her, for the one thing she still needs. She's led outside to smoke and falls asleep on a bench after the overexertion, something to do with losing the flask.

I've tried everything with her, says our father, now sitting up in bed. I don't want you accusing me of neglect.

What enigmatic dumb thing can we say to clue him in that we're all sympathy? He doesn't hear anything straight, and certainly not anything to do with dependency, a circle like that. Is there a god to do with grain and fermentation that we might get somewhere with? says the oldest. He likes grain, anything in farmer talk. Farmer talk and god might get through to him.

God is barley, says the last.

Osiris, an Egyptian drunken god, says another. We'll have a service.

He needs to rest, says the nurse.

Chain after chain of restaurants encircle our evening exit. Let us eat, we tell each other, as in a litany, one we ourselves can answer.

One of us does not sleep in the half-night of the TV he refuses to turn down or turn off. This one is lucky to spot, in the gray of that light, the matching gray in her father's face that no nurse would have noticed from down the end of the long hall where they hide. She presses the button, then goes out into the hall and fetches these nurses, more than one. Tubes are found and pressed into service with bags of this and that on the end, a cup and a pill. When his color returns, he thanks the nurses. I could have died, he says, except for the nurses. One of us reminds him who called them but he says to the assembled as soon as she steps out the door for a possible nap, the nurses saved me.

Time to go, he says, surgery smergery, he says, paying our mother's hotel bill.

You should stay at least a day to rest, we say. Our planes leave in a day.

The father looks at the mother. I am tired of waiting, she says, as if waiting were another old dress, one of those lying on the floor of her room to be rid of.

Left behind, we tour the city: its flatness, its buses, the shop windows full of us and our faces. We laugh at menus offering food combinations so inedible they have to be Midwestern, and even try on clothes we'll never wear. A fire sale, says one of us. They should be burned.

We walk home to our hotel in the near dark, in the rain, the prairie dogs stalwart beside their holes, the plague in abatement, the we in false recovery.

SECONDS

Seconds, or cranberry surprise? She's his sister-in-law, she can baby him.

Of course, Dad says. Both.

More gravy appears, potatoes, peas and carrots, the surprise.

She says she doesn't know what's keeping him, he hates cold food.

Dad moves the gravy around so it floods his plate. It's a warm Thanksgiving, he says, as if that has something to do with his brother being a hour late.

She fills his glass with red until he says he had white. Then she doles out so much whipped cream he actually spoons it back.

Her daughter-in-law leaves the table to tend the baby on the living room floor.

The second cousin, really just somebody they scrounged up to make light talk, says in all the eating of seconds and drinking of thirds and the spooning of dessert, How has his treatment been going?

He was happy enough checking out his new ranch yesterday, says his son. Won a bet from me on how long it would take me to learn the new irrigation system.

They drink, they eat.

Can't say we didn't wait, says the wife, showing them a blackened sweet potato.

They file from the table to the TV, the dishes stay on the table. Don't do them, says Dad. It'll make him feel bad.

I don't mind, she says, not sitting down on the couch, veering back to the sink. You can do them later.

Dad likes that, the joke of him washing up. He asks the baby if she wants her toes eaten, and pulls at each digit to make her laugh. Her mother gathers her back when she kicks but she writhes out of her arms for her daddy, who's searching the stations for football or parade.

Dad slow-foots it to the lounger. There's gravy on his white shirt and darkness across his face. He scratches the side of his nose after he's settled and points at the cabinet on the wall. Wasn't there something in there?

The son sees the gap, the one empty rack. Sometimes he cleans it, he says.

His mother's in the kitchen, washing the pans, but listening. Water still running, she comes to the door.

Where? says her son, pointing at the rack.

She has no idea. The child cries and no one picks her up.

Dad says, Try the long barn.

The child hiccups her crying while the cousin says surely he's just driving around for air, a ride to calm him down for all the holiday celebrating or to see if a gate is shut—everything everyone's said twice already. Why that barn?

I don't know, says Dad. But don't you check, he says to the son when he goes for the coat closet. Call Pete to go with you.

The son is shaking now, a big-frame shake that usually with him is a sign of anger but not now. You call Pete, he says, I'm going. He puts the keys in his pocket, skips the closet for the door.

No, says his mother, into the room in two steps. No, you don't.

Shit, says the son. It's Thanksgiving. He's supposed to—

Wait, says Dad. I hear something.

They listen to what? The car door of a neighbor, a little too much booze in the slam? Nothing. But in the interim Dad whips out his phone, he 911s.

As if such a call could solve something, the others listen. Of course 911 isn't local, no Pete they can get reassurance from, just a recital of regulations: Missing Persons aren't missing for at least a day. No help at all.

She punches in numbers on her own phone. Her daughter-in-law passes her with the baby on the way to the kitchen, the baby tapping her arm, a comfort motion.

Pete says he'll come over, she says, he says he hasn't had enough turkey.

We won't see Pete for another hour, says the son still at the front door. Pete has money on the game.

I said it's important, says the wife.

You don't want to go, says Dad in a voice that says he doesn't either.

You stay here, says his mother. His wife agrees, the baby sucking at her bottle, she forbids him.

Did he take his pills today? the son asks. Now plaid-coated, he's the image of his father, just about as wrinkled, and just as stubborn.

Of course, says his mother.

But did he swallow them?

How can I tell? She turns to face the kitchen door, she just turns.

Dad closes his eyes. Wait, he says.

It's about two minutes later that Pete's car pulls up and Dad pumps the lounger upright. Of course they all hope it's not Pete. That would mean what they sense could be true. The son runs to the door and out to where the two of them, Pete and the son, talk and then leave without a hello or anything to anybody else.

Dad plays with the baby, a peekaboo that she likes, then cries about, Dad's peek is too shrill and his mother too desperate for calm. She should take the baby home but she can't.

The dishes are done.

A car parks in the drive just ten minutes later, and all of them inside are out on the carport coatless. The son says Pete's called the coroner, the son says he didn't go in but when he enters the living room, dropping the keys while trying to repocket them, his face isn't his father's anymore, it's bent, it's creased and drained. He's seen what he's seen.

Mom, says the son. Mom.

She has backed up back into the house and is crossing one arm over her chest, then the next, and the sound she makes wakes up the baby. If you'd only—sooner.

He shakes his head. After holding his mother and then holding his wife, he says to Dad, How did you know?

Dad says he guessed. He liked that long barn. Sooner or later, he says. He had it in him.

The baby reaches for her father and he takes her just as his wife moves away. Together they almost drop her.

HOT RAIN

In July, Dad notices on his clinic printout that he has stage four kidney failure. His doctor hadn't told him. Despite Dad having had a bad heart for twenty years, he yells at me and then hangs up when I hesitate to swap his kidney for mine. He'll be ninety next week.

He leaves messages with my sibs, with similar results. How are you feeling about this kidney problem? is how the youngest, the cleverest, copes with his question. I'll bet you're scared.

I'm not, says Dad. I'm mad.

He's got the money to buy a new one, but not even quack doctors in Asia will take an order—he's tried online. Rebuffed but still signed in, he shops for a bride instead. He can't get his credit card number in right. He finds his checkbook and decides to put nine thousand dollars into his caregiver's checking account to sweeten a marriage proposal, then tells her he'll fire her if she doesn't take the money and sleep with him. She refuses, but keeps the money. He fires her anyway when she won't help him go to a pawn shop to buy another gun.

Her mistake is to try reasoning with him. You have six guns already, she says, why waste your money? A rifle with a scope, three shotguns, a pistol, and a revolver.

I can never find them, he says. They're not handy. He doesn't know she's moved all of them to a safe in a storage unit, he's forgotten he's just fired her.

It's a phase, says the doctor. He doesn't say *dementia*. He tells her to hide not just the guns, but the knives too. He doesn't say whether he's worried about murder or suicide.

It's hard to shake hands with a guy in a straitjacket, let alone hug him hello, I say to my sister on the phone the week before we arrive for his big birthday party. She says it's even harder to do it when you're bleeding from an ice pick or a scissors.

I sigh, a kind of complicity.

The witch might come to the party, she says, you remember—the caregiver he's already given the house to for some kind of sex. Not the one who took the money.

A year earlier, we were so happy to have the witch as an aide, as thick-hipped, godawful ugly-mouthed, -faced, and -handed as she was. Not to mention quick on the fabrication. She did take him to music nights at the café, she put in a first-rate sit-down shower, she baled his hay for fun, she did not balk at going on a cruise with him to anywhere. It was on one to Alaska that no one had known about, when Dad came down with a 105 fever and had to be airlifted to a hospital, that worry began to surface. The sudden redecoration of his house at great expense also caught our attention. I'm giving it to her, no problem, said Dad. That's when we started to seriously visit.

If the witch shows up at the birthday party, she will be difficult. I've always thought of *will* as a promising verb, I sigh again into the phone, not this noun that has to be forever babysat. There are already seven of us to consider with his noun. I tell my sister there's no future in that verb at all anymore, and dead air hangs on the phone, deader than before. She begs me to fly in early and spell her, but I make an excuse. Other sibs' excuses, she tells me, are not as lame as mine. Check him into the hospital the whole weekend before the party, I tell her. Tell him it's his kidney, I suggest.

He doesn't trust me to tie his shoes.

Play the six-hour cowboy cable series. That will give him time for a good nap.

He'll just get more wired, says my sister. He's not sleeping at night anymore, he sleeps while I drive him around or cook dinner, he's fresh while I'm worn out. He woke me at three a.m. to ask if I would sleep with him. I almost said I would, just to get some sleep.

Incest is like asking for a kidney, I say.

Ha, ha, ha, she laughs in huffs, all faux. Dad's putting us on speakerphone.

Hi, Dad, I say. How tall is the corn?

He says Warren Buffet didn't buy corn this year. He put his money into transplants. Transplants, he repeats in case I think he's talking about some other kind of plant.

He calls back to tell me Warren Buffet should have married his wife sooner. The tax consequences alone, he exclaims. I'm writing an editorial for the newspaper all about it. Then he's onto his kidney again, complaining about our lack of compassion. What'll it be next time, I don't say, an arm, a ventricle, my synapses? While I'm thinking it's enough just to listen, he hangs up again.

I don't call my sister back that weekend. I know one of the caregivers will return in twelve hours, so her wait will be a kind of late summer thriller deadline where helicopters should be hovering. I take half a sleeping pill instead of worrying, I save the other half to give to my sister at his birthday party.

Dad and I are rounding the first corner of the block, foot by foot. It's my vigil, months earlier. Do women still like the big flashy ones? asks Dad.

What do I know? I never went for much of a ring.

You were a grass widow that last time, Dad says, eyeing the break in the sidewalk he has to negotiate. Divorcees don't merit big rocks. Begging your pardon, he says, but not taking it back.

I give him a shoulder's worth of boost up a curb, and we pass the next door neighbor's open garage. We are not clear of the opening when the neighbor calls from out of its recesses: I thought you were dead.

I'm flattered, says Dad. To be thought alive.

I mean, says the man who has interrupted a troweling, the implement wet and cement on his pant leg, you weren't in church yesterday.

Nice of you to notice, says Dad, shoving his feet forward.

They keep track? I whisper, out of eye range if not ear, since Dad's volume is way up on his hearing aid.

He sweeps his hand over the lawn-green perspective, so staid and kept, and shouts: So what if I don't go to church now and then? I'll show them the flames of hell.

I look back, and the neighbor is just now retreating with his trowel.

We walk farther down the block and stop under a blooming catalpa. Stinks up the place, says Dad, inhaling its perfume deep. Another good excuse to rest, he says, and he leans against its bark.

Who would be the recipient of this aforementioned flashy diamond? I ask, endeavoring to talk away the slowness of our progress, struggling to make the question sound interest-free.

Dad rubs his grizzled face. I haven't shaved for two days. That's a hint, he says. She's good with a razor.

I make an eye-rolling sound, a smothered chuckle. I don't call her the witch to his face. The caregiver you took to Alaska?

I guess, says Dad. Unless you and her sisters sent me a few more to review.

You've got a second one.

She cleans the house, he says. Since we are stopped again anyway, the whole long block and another corner of it looming, Dad pats his jacket and his pants pocket and his inside pocket until at last he produces a ring. Four thousand dollars, he says, cracking the jeweler's nut of a box hard with his fingers until it opens and the ring flings itself into the adjacent grass.

I'm bad-backed but I swoop down and trap the little glitter in my fingers like an insect. Nice, I say.

I got the house girl to take me to the ring store after my acupuncture. Dad's chicanery turns him suddenly shy and he doesn't say more.

I stow the ring back into its box. The witch gives two-hour baths with salts and then powders his toes. We gave her the name after we accused Dad of being bewitched. I propel him forward, past the sprays of an offending sprinkler. What if she doesn't take the ring?

Dad stops. Why the hell wouldn't she?

Just saying, I say, taking a few steps past him. Just in case. Think about it. She's half your age. She'll put you in a home and leave you there.

Dad thinks that is hilarious it's so unlikely. I'm going to play sick and have her stay over. Then at three a.m., I'll climb into bed with her.

That's a plan, I say. On the other hand, what will you do if she says yes?

You sound like a damn shrink, says Dad. He plants his feet firm and looks around. A lot of robins out.

We talk about robins.

I guess I'd feel sad if she didn't say yes, he says after the robins fly off. All I've got is money. Then he says nothing and removes his glasses, rubs his eyes.

It takes until the birds return to the tree to get him going again.

We play cards and Dad wins. Two scotches later, we inspect his indoor pool: a long crack in the dry cement at one end, leaves from the house next door at the bottom of the other. She comes at eight in the morning, he says with a grin. I'm always up by four.

She could have her own boyfriend, I say. Doesn't she?

She lives with a Patterson. A cowboy Patterson. He doesn't move fast enough for her.

I see, I say, watching him move. As I recall, those people like to crack heads.

So?

She could be teasing you. Caregivers like to tease, what else do they have to do? I finish the drink in my hand.

She'd look good in a bathing suit, says Dad, raising his glass to the pool.

I'm sure, I say. Although *good* isn't the word I'd use in this instance. You'll have to get that fixed, I say, about the crack.

Why? says Dad. I'm just about dead.

You've got plans, I say.

Call the contractor, says Dad, throwing up his hands in excitement.

If I get down on one knee, the fire department will have to come and jerk me to my feet again, he says after a long talk about a bad thriller he'd seen.

You'd better practice, I say, stupidly egging him on.

But what if she says no, I say again, hauling him and myself off the floor in a fit of laughter.

I'll die happy I tried, says Dad.

Dad has the witch dress him in a suit with a shirt that takes a tie. You'll just stain it, she says, buttoning all those buttons, fetching the tie. Where are you off to, anyway?

Nowhere, he answers. He loves having her this close is what he's told me, tying the tie, he'd endure a week of formal dress to get her breasts to almost touch his chest like this. The witch has bathed him with a bottlebrush, or at least a wash rag on a stick for the crevices, and all the while he imagined her hand on him. Her shirt is buttoned but not quite to the top, and when she leans down to clip his suspenders in place, he must have seen darkness.

He is so thrilled he falls asleep before she does up his shoes.

I smile at him at breakfast but he just eats his bacon. He says no to cream and no to blueberries. The witch goes off to make his bed. I open the paper between us and read out the headlines. Dad grunts as if he's listening. When she returns, he taps my paper and raises his eyebrows. I have to go to the post office, I say, and do you need anything mailed?

Femaled, says Dad.

She says, you two are so funny.

Dad doesn't laugh.

When I get back, Dad is sleeping in his La-Z-Boy, his necktie curled in his fingers and his collar open. The ring box sits on the table, closed but looking left behind. The witch is wiping the counter where she's spilled medicine. She is upset, her face red, her wiping wild. Did you know what he was up to?

Well, I say, the way the incriminated do.

They are always asking, she says. I get offers all the time, at least once a week. You know, she says, turning to me, I'll take just the house.

My sister, who shows up after I go home, can't find the painting. It's French, sailboats at the quay, thick impasto, signed and valuable. What the witch has hung in its place is a reproduction of a powerboat, V's of gulls overhead, water plowed, framed by lighter wallpaper screaming *gone* around it. A few other items are missing, a clock, a silver pitcher, two glass birds. Mom kept a lot of stuff on display so it's hard to keep track. Beside the powerboat is a photo of Dad, newly taken. When he wakes up, it's the first thing he sees. Who is that white-headed fool at the end of the bed looking down at me? If he doesn't have dementia, this photo would trigger it. This is what I suggest to my sister when she calls with her painting discovery, and all the other new changes. By moving things around, the witch puts him out of control, off guard because what he sees is no longer familiar.

Dad says the painting's in the basement but it's not, my sister tells me. There's a locked hall closet.

Well, unlock it. It'll only take a table knife or a credit card.

I've tried. It's something more complicated.

Call the locksmith.

The witch would flip out. She's territorial. And Dad would back her up. You know what he said when I suggested she might polish the silver? Sell it at a yard sale.

My sister calls me again two days later. More paintings have disappeared. The place looks like an institution, she says. Bare walls. What she puts in their places you can buy by the lot. And she's taken down the drapes. Says it helps him remember where he is when he can see the tree.

He hates trees, and he can still tell you where to turn in the middle of a snowstorm.

Soon Christmas is upon us, the season of giving and giving up, of abandoning all hope, of realigning oneself with one's relatives. I fly back to spell the holiday with my sister, and there it is: no painting here and here and here. I try the knob on the closet door that is locked. Did you ask her for a key?

It's not that the witch won't give it; she says she doesn't have it, says my sister. She knows nothing about a key. But neither does Dad. He just looks sly when I ask.

But what if what's missing is stolen? I ask Dad.

Dad hates thieves. The bane of capitalism, let alone the socialism he says we are always going on about. He says, Call the cops, if that's what you think. Instead, my sister and I decide to Nancy Drew the situation but we have to wait until the witch exits. She likes to fill up his water glass with vodka, select the whiny country songs she likes to listen to while she gets him dinner.

We know how to cook, we tell her. He has favorites we can make.

She lays rubber leaving.

After he's bedded to the blaring TV, we set to work on the hinges with a screwdriver. We use a headlamp to do it because if he sees the light on, he'll insist on it off, to save electricity. Television, on all night, apparently uses no electricity. The lack of light makes it dicey when it comes to the actual removal of the door, at least in the avoiding-dropping-it-on-one-of-our-toes part. I drop it on my sister's, who is directing my twisting. What's a sister for? I say after her squeak of pain, but I'm already pointing my headlamp into the closet.

Five paintings, stacked. Various glass items, ceramic birds, my mother's silver talcum shaker. Did Dad forget that he gave her the key? What's going on? Why is she doing this?

To drive me crazy, says my sister. To drive me away. She knows Dad won't say anything, that I'm the only one who cares.

She's sobbing now. Maybe it has to do with her foot as well as her heart. I pat her arm as if it's an appendage I've never noticed before. We are not great huggers.

In the morning Dad is angry about the unhinged door. He is not delighted that we have recovered the paintings. He says put them in the bank vault if they're so valuable. But Dad, we say, why not just hang them back up?

I didn't okay this, says Dad and the witch frowns, calls up our brother, the one who hired her.

She's protecting all of you, says my brother. The assets.

By hiding the paintings?

I know plot, which is just a shortened form of conspiracy theory. The witch and my brother are in it together. He refuses to hire a second person for her days off, nobody should interfere with her care of Dad. After all, she keeps Dad out of my brother's hair; he is, after all, living in the same town full time, working with Dad for the last thirty years.

My sister flies home two days early.

It does seem my brother is in cahoots with the witch because when I suggest, in deference to visiting small grandchildren running around, that misplaced and relocated furniture be moved, the witch calls him and he threatens to beat up anybody who moves anything.

I tell Dad on another walk around the block that he's caught between a gold digger and a madman. About my brother he says nothing, but about the witch he says, what about her references? Not that he's checked them. I do and one is from a school friend of mine who is dead. A day later, I receive an email from that friend's sister-in-law saying the witch was fired for seducing the husband. Then I do a little more research: her sisters had to sue her over the custody of her own father. Apparently she let him wander.

Also she's been arrested for shooting without a license. It's bad enough she has a gun, I say to Dad but he's not impressed. Girls need guns, he says. Why don't you have one?

You ought to come to New York for New Year's, I counter. I throw in my highest card: there's a bar that specializes in bowl games from the Midwest.

He pretends to perk up when really he's been thinking about it all along.

I doctor Dad fast in the darkness of a winter morning: diabetic shot, hearing aids, heart pills. The witch's arrival is imminent, she likes to control his every waking moment. I drive the two of us at top speed out of town, despite ice, and the ice coming down.

Miles later, we breakfast in glamor, eggs Benedict doubled, while Dad's cell phone rings through every chew. My brother or the witch? They work in tandem, their numbers flashing on the marquee of the phone that Dad doesn't answer. I'm surprised he agreed to the trip, but then there's nothing like sneaking around, being the center of attention. Last year when a journalist came to interview me for a local magazine, Dad wouldn't stop talking. When it was time for a picture, he popped his head in. That night at our hotel he gets twisted in his T-shirt and wrenches his shoulder and curses our trip until I cut the shirt off him. Later, I'm called a kidnapper by my brother, but during the flight and a week of theater and suppers and naps, our father behaves like a kid and enjoys it.

He fires the witch the day before his flight back. I am surprised by that too, if his goal is really romancing women.

Then there's his birthday party.

By the time we wend our way—rise at five a.m., drive to the airport, wait on the tarmac for an hour, fly four hours, deplane to wait four hours for a shuttle that drops us off at the truck stop four more hours later, then drive to the pre-birthday party family picnic and bonfire at the lake house—I am not prepared for family revelation. My husband, who did not like the sound of *birthday surprise* that Dad has hinted at, has accompanied me. Already it turns out that one sibling out of the seven has been quizzed by Dad about why she's shown up. Because I love you, she answered. She cut off his speech about taking all his money.

He seems to have forgotten about his kidneys. I'm driving him home from the ashes of the bonfire when he says he has something very important to tell me.

I park in his driveway. I file into his office behind him. Look at how spry he is! He could beat me around the block now, his secret must pour energy into him like a regular pep pill. He takes a seat behind the big cluttered mess of a table

I always winnow when I show up, and I take the crying seat, where clients of his used to lay out their legal problems. He doesn't give me time to take out a handkerchief, he blurts out that he wants me to return all the corporate shares of his family farm so he can give the proceeds to "single women with children," or to his alma mater, or else to the witch, even if she is fired. Maybe the library would like all the money. Okay? he says. Single women?

I stare at the reproduction of Wyeth behind his head, the one where the crippled woman has a long way to crawl before she gets to the farmhouse.

All the women you have any contact with are single women with children, I say, is that a coincidence? Or are you making up for when my sister and I were single women with children and you gave us nothing?

A half a beat of lightning flashes between us, metaphorical but literal enough. Get out of the house, he shouts.

It is eleven p.m. I hide in the far bedroom while my sister talks him down, tucks him in, turns off his light. I find half of the sleeping pill I've hoarded for her and she drives herself back to the lake house to take it.

I soon find out why she's not sleeping in the house. Dad flicks on my light at three a.m., holding a long kitchen knife. Where are they? he asks.

Who? I say from under the covers.

The guys who cut the lawn.

I move not too quickly toward the drapes under the bright light, I open them to the black outside and I point, They're almost done. They'll be here again in the morning.

My husband is pretending to sleep in the other single bed. I am angry he's not defending me, yes, but if I scream for him, what will Dad do? Let's go back to your room, I say.

Dad's frowning, silent, standing with the knife at his side as if that's what you carry with your pajamas, an accessory. Can't you fit that in the dishwasher? I say when we pass the kitchen.

He says that will make it dull.

They'll be here in the morning? You're sure? he says to me from his bed, with four pocket knives open beside the big one peeking out of his covers.

I glance out the window en route to my room. The lawn can't be cut any shorter.

My husband is sitting up, the light on, when I get back. He says everything is fine. Or it will be in the morning. Delusions are nighttime events. Don't take anything your dad says after seven seriously.

But he hooks a chair back under the doorknob.

In the morning Dad announces to me and the rest of the assembled that he's suing us with all the money he makes from the family farm, every one of us will be sued for not giving our shares to him, making us pay lawyers for years that only he can afford. Thanks for all those years I didn't have to pay so much in corporate tax, he says, but now he wants total control. He will sue us right into the grave and beyond. You can do that, he says. You can keep on suing.

He's smiling, giving us the news.

But Dad, we say, we've spent all of the last year taking care of you in rotation, leaving our jobs and children and responsibilities, and staying with you like nursemaids, preventing the witch from robbing you blind.

I paid your airfare, he says.

Three hours before his birthday party, cousin Phil drives up in his red Corvette, a model with shiny hubcaps that glitter, a car that radiates wealth. His father distributed all of his estate to each of his children and then committed suicide. It was a sure sign he was sick, Dad insists.

Take me for a ride, he tells Phil. It is difficult to wedge him inside, his thick torso is hard to bend and position in a seat that low, it takes two men to lever him out. By then he's beaming. We went a hundred on a back road, he says, as if he pressed that pedal himself.

Dad could have just been a guy who had a lot of sex with my mother and made money, the man who bragged to his friends that he did not pay for my education or any of my weddings. He inherited land from his father, a Depression-era real estate dealer and manure-spreader salesman, and the G. I. Bill paid for his legal education. He loves pretty girls—my hold is slipping in this category—and horse races, Cadillacs, and a tall glass of vodka. So what if he's a person and not the god I remembered. I went to whatever school I could pay for and kept on marrying anyway—I was free, free to live my own life and not obey him, that first tenet of fealty between children and parent. So why do I think he owes me now? I must have gotten misty in the brain when I flew out to help him every few months, cooked his meals, drove him around, and played so much gin rummy, hand after hand. He watched my cleavage like any other guy.

Am I having these thoughts? No, I am sobbing. Heaves of sobs and tears but not too many, I am too angry. Destroyed. I mean nothing to Dad; that is the revelation. I am standing with this revelation, no, I am squatting. An old lady like me in a squat? The ground is right there, the dirt of it against the back of a barn. I flathand myself to standing and wipe my face dry.

Dad and my siblings are lined up inside this faux barn, waiting to order. It is a restaurant but also the site of slaughter, I pass a corral of cows to the right of the door purported to be organic, mouthing what looks like rubber. They could be eating each other.

The siblings smile to see me. They have all had their own audience and resemble me in my extreme state, variously affected, although not sobbing outside the barn, which I don't admit to, no. I smile back, but they are nonetheless grim in their rictus, in their *I'll have the fries.*

For we must eat. No one has it in them to cook or even shop or worse, leftover-up a meal in this, the late afternoon before the party. Starvation is possible and Dad must be fed. Fuel for ourselves is also necessary—someone must call lawyers or decide not to, someone must make new reservations to leave sooner. I can see the flight in all of them: four around the booth and a fifth flown to the bathroom to tidy up. Tears there too, triggered not by sadness but anger.

No one could have imagined this change in him, his utter rejection of us. As a father, maybe he's out of practice. We were gone after he became a judge, when he boasted about reading the fine print, when to fight, how long people could take it. A bellyache of his could get a guy more jail time, is what he told us after he retired. He wasn't someone who came to the prom and took pictures, nor even graduation, but he'd slip you a fifty on your way back to campus, he had someone order cakes for everyone at Christmas. His charm is bifold— that is, he extends it to cover the moment. Quip is his best weapon, quick quips that show even he, with few hairs still screwed to his head, is still present and accounted for.

Fries arrive. No one is supposed to eat them. Diseases of the heart run in the family (isn't that Dad's real problem?) but now is the self-erasing moment, the tack of pleasure, the tasteless potatoes and grease taken into our mouths like a sacrament. Where's the ketchup? We are ungrateful and unworthy, Dad is telling us, beaming as if he's just discovered the true meaning of being a parent. At our age he figures we don't need to be coddled, protected from the truth the way we were in our upbringing, not acknowledging all his years of upbringing-neglect, the true truth.

He did feed us, we were fed; that was costly.

Half a sandwich later I can almost talk. Across from me sits Dad. He's finished, but eyeing my fries as if they have just fallen off his plate.

It is not the money we bemoan in particular, and I think I can speak for my siblings in this, in our angry despair. Our thin wallets will not expand like an artery, no, the heart is the site of our suffering the parent's withdrawal at this late date, the redrawing of the role that reaches, it seems, all the way back to where, as actual children, we thought we were lucky in love, given such an awful mother. She smoked too much to use her ivory cigarette holder often, she loved good clothes and food, but only for herself, her own mother dining in a feathered hat every night on a chop made just for her. When our mother died, leaving nothing to us but one token coat to a sibling so we would know that she hadn't forgotten the possibility, we were not surprised. She insisted, as soon as we were old enough—is there an age?—she never wanted us. Since by then we had children, we had insight into that want; the raising is hard. But she never mentioned the joy. I wasted my life, she told us before she died. She must not have wanted to waste her death.

We get it now—we're not getting anything from either of them. All that time in the past we were puppets charmed by this pretend Dad schtick into the roles of multiple pie-maker, clucking watchmen, and harried caretakers, nay, just coworkers at his mercy, without benefit of love or money.

Okay, if we can't have love, it's the money.

Of course we had the vague outlines before of these lines that he spoke to us, we say in the car after lunch, going back to the house where we grew up and began to finish this growing, where we will pack for a hotel or a plane just as soon as the party is over. We are not sniveling adolescents, surprising parents in a bedroom, but the knowledge of someone you're in love with for so long turning out to be not so enamored of you makes a person mostly rethink yourself. Who is, deep down, at fault? At base line, *who we are* has a crack running through it, one side the lovable, on the other some non-Freudian integer or unentangled mitochondria, some heart, smoking and cracked.

Finally, the party. Surprise! We have to pay for the whole of the town to feast at this party, Dad's new idea, although he's the only one who can afford it. We can't disagree; we've already put it on our cards, assuming reimbursement. Several of us will have to take out loans to cover it. As the townspeople file in, I wonder: Have any of them endured rogue elders? Is this another secret they're keeping until we're old enough? The doctor coming in late admits at last, *sotto voce,* Dad's only a little demented, no problem. What about the guns and the knives? I whisper-shriek. What about all those checks he's writing?

He's writing a check to the doctor for a hospital wing that needs one.

When it comes time to sing the required praises after our paid-for dinner of fish or beef, and no other sibling will approach the podium, as shocked as we all are, I stand, because who am I except the eldest and noisiest? But all that comes out of my mouth is a story about how, in a blizzard, in an airport without money or credit card, I woke him with a call for help and he said find Traveler's Aid and I said you are Traveler's Aid and he laughed. Made you strong, he says from his seat on the dais and the audience—all of them thinking they know everything about everyone—they think the story is so funny. You kids don't live here anymore, their laughing suggests. You don't pledge our allegiance, check out our library books, pump our gas. You get to fly away; you deserve airports like that.

At daylight we look at each other standing in the hallway with our bags and our half-made reservations. The airlines can take us but only as far as Minneapolis and the look we have is a question posed: Is there among us one with machinations, someone with a heartlessness similar to Dad's? We can't have that kind of fault now or our father will crush us entirely, he will win if we are divided, and there we will be, all of us sobbing behind the barn, less one. We count heads: not the buxom food taster whose job depends on being as sharp as her last broken test tube, not the squishy middle girl, happy at a wheel, car or pot's, not the environmental lady lawyer who always wants advice, not the dashing brother smooth as butter, designing puppets.

We know who it is—that brother in cahoots with the witch—and we don't honk when we pass his place in exit.

Outside my apartment I watch people cross the street. I'll bet some of them have parents who want to keep everything too, money and love. Why haven't I heard about this power problem before? Why do I think the end is all hearts and flowers when I know the beginning—the birthing at least—is agony, and the next few weeks after are blessed with love hormonally induced and sleep-deprived obedience. How else could you endure it? Love kicks in.

This is love kicked out. I suppose everyone would keep the hand they are dealt with if they could, *me daughter you dad,* but the cards' values are more unstable than that. The King of Hearts turned Club.

A week after the birthday, we lawyer up.

A month later the witch doesn't turn Dad's car into the driveway until four p.m. My husband and I have waited hours in a car parked down the street. We have searched for him at the bank, the drive-in, the library, the car wash, even the cemetery, every quarter hour another ratchet up of nervousness. We even drive to the dump with its new owners, the dump looking homemade now, a forest of swing sets, towers of tires, new plastic bags ghosting the property. I jump at a grasshopper that pings the car between car wrecks. After we leave, I eat corn chips, chocolate, cherries with pits, then burritos at Dad's favorite café, sitting way back by the dishwasher, but he doesn't show to take a seat, and afterwards, driving and parking down the street, my husband doesn't nap, a feat of unusual vigilance. We're in a movie stakeout but the plot has faltered, the suspense has sagged, but then—I call the sheriff to tell him Dad's getting out of his pickup. The sheriff won't let us serve the papers alone. They like to have guns, he says, the ones who get served.

Knowing Dad's penchant for weapons, I say, okay, I say fine.

We ring the doorbell, something I've never done before. The witch answers, sees the sheriff, skitters elsewhere. Dad knows immediately what the papers are about. He turns to my husband and tells him how he's beating the sorghum market.

The sheriff smiles, says he's never seen anybody as gentle as I am, explaining why temporary custody is important and necessary and can't be avoided. I explain until I turn blue, my father enjoying my struggle, while the sheriff and his sidekick stand in the hall, their hands on their holsters.

At five a.m. the next morning, there's an ambulance at the door. Dad says his heart hurts him.

Why didn't you wake me? I say, putting a hat over his grizzled hair, finding his jacket. I could've just driven you. I'm your guardian.

You don't care about me.

I find his medication, let the dog out, check his blood sugar level and pack food, as if he's going to camp. He doesn't like the food at the hospital. We ride five minutes in the ambulance. Emergency greets him like an old friend; they have his room ready.

Home again, Dad wakes two hours earlier than the night before. I hear talk and find the sheriff in the kitchen. I couldn't get my cell phone to work, says Dad. What if it were an emergency?

The sheriff understands. He turns up the volume on Dad's phone while Dad says, Don't you think my kids ought to be happy with what they got from me? I gave them life, he says.

The sheriff shakes his head as if there's something wrong with his hearing, not Dad's, and leaves. Dad dials the ambulance.

Soon enough my brother's wife kneels in front of my father. She has six ovens and has plans for more. I can see her through Dad's French doors, which she has slammed shut and locked. What is she is saying to him that he nods to? Where does he think she is leading him when she takes him by the hand?

I'm sorry, I have custody, I tell her at the front door. You can't just take him.

She takes him anyway, and an extra shirt.

The lawyer says wait four hours for them to return him. She's packed none of his medication. I email and text my brother, I telephone and no one picks up. After four hours, the lawyer says Call the sheriff.

The sheriff brings him home, sputtering and furious. When my brother bursts through the door behind him, his ten-year-old daughter trains a camera on me. You watch your step, she snarls.

The next day I don't spend half the afternoon making Dad meatloaf, I buy frozen.

His doctor, the one my father is giving a wing to, my brother's friend, says my brother has to leave his own home and come live with us. That's what Dad wants. The doctor says we can reconcile that way. His idea. I can't not live with Dad, I have custody. Temporary temporary custody, my brother reminds me. Don't bother to get comfy.

My husband and I are sitting on the grass under the shade of a light pole on day twelve. The town has cut down all the trees to make the park easier to mow. It's a real park though—there is a big public waste container to one side of the pole. The grass is so hot, we crouch under the single strip of shade that light pole makes, we chew and we swallow. Even if the sandwich were other than tasteless, it's not really eating. We could be dogs, ripping up the grass to vomit.

It's not like you don't love him, says my husband.

It's not like I do, I say back.

After we return for our shift, we discover I am released. The paper Dad holds at the door proclaims that my brother has what I had, temporary custody. We must leave everything to him.

Patio-lightning, patio-rain, both so hot. Yet I shiver. The white plastic-you-know-the-chair I set over the rails of the sliding door so my feet get wet, but not my bottle. I've found one beer in the fridge of the lake house we're waiting in until it's time for the dawn drive to the airport, the house the brother installed a new lock on that we must jimmy open. My husband's nursing his half of the beer in a glass in the dark inside it.

All this nice warm rain, like piss. Like being pissed on. Such a thing could happen with leakage from a bad kidney.

Stop making excuses, the husband says from the kitchen.

A psychologist is to decide whether Dad is demented and needs any custodianship at all. Demented is not the diagnosis my brother wants, given the timing of the gift of a whole section of land. Rather than interview me the way she has the other sibs, the psychologist tells me my brother has raged at her, hearing her diagnosis, and what am I going to do about this rage? I say Dad is sick, he's the one who should be taken care of. A week later, after enduring more raging and my sister-in-law's begging, she recants her diagnosis, she tells the judge there's no problem. Even I know that dementia is peek-a-boo, that symptoms can be suppressed.

Now no one has custody.

Not long after, I am back in the state, and telling an audience everything I know about a famous dead writer they love, and how I am like the dead writer and deserve the same love. I make them laugh but I only sell three books. I think delivering that talk will be the hardest part of the gig but in the very back row of the audience sit my bad brother and Dad.

My fast-beating heart veers my brain into paranoia: he is ambushing me, having found a way to rattle me into incoherence, which would not only ruin the evening but derail my career and who knows? make me give up being an artist. All families who have in their midst an artist harbor this flickering support. *Why are they so special and not me?* And not just sibling rivalry but paternal—*I could have been an artist if I hadn't been a parent.* Of course they could pretend that nothing at all has happened between us, of course time could be bent so as to avoid what happens when a man refuses to consider he won't be around forever. He walks past me.

Two years later my sister-in-law takes Dad to the doctor. It is three days before my sibs and I and my brother are going to sign an irrevocable trust that divides everything equitably. The lawyers have discovered my father has tax problems, and moving the corporate shares will eliminate them, thus no love will have to be lost or extended. And my bad brother will still get twice as much as everyone else. Nevertheless, my sister-in-law is unhappy. How many more ovens could she buy with the entire estate? She tells their friend, the doctor, that Dad is now truly demented and needs stronger medication immediately. Although Dad says no to the doctor, I am not, her begging job works. He writes a prescription for a strong antipsychotic that Dad must take, or must be persuaded to take, regardless of its effect on his heart.

At the signing, each faction has its lawyer or lawyers, six altogether, and we all sit in separate rooms with our wants and our needs, with a mediator flitting between us, our pens ready for autographing our part of the paper that says it's a trust that we're sealing. Trust? The legal industry is all about trust, the point of having the expensive lawyers is to enforce it. At least the witch is not here. Adult Protective Services hauled her off about a month ago as a result of alienation from my brother. Since no one talks to anyone now without legal counsel, who knows what she did to forfeit her by now completely redecorated house.

Hours into the negotiations, the mediator strongly advises that we each meet with Dad to apologize to him for having tried to deprive him of power. I struggle with calmness, I listen to the mediator trying to put over his Hallmark idea, that we will all join hands, I am calm, and then I am not, I am too damaged to kneel at the feet of the patriarch. Head bowed, sobbing, I run from the room to the car we have parked in the lot.

The lawyer sends the other side our undying love, and our willingness to sign whatever, gambling that this will do. The truth is Dad is grandstanding the humiliation part. He takes his time and takes a nap while we wait in our rooms for hours.

Then he signs. Once the paper is safe inside our lawyer's briefcase, Dad says, My god, a couple of days ago, I almost died from those pills your sister-in-law said were so important.

The lake house is destroyed by fire. So appropriate: the scene of our retreat. My brother moves away and leaves my father to manage the farm all by himself. *Take that,* is what this means, *you didn't give me everything.*

I remember patting the top of Dad's head at the hospital in an attempt at consolation, flattening his few fine wisps of hair to his pink skull. It was one of the many times he called the ambulance to pick him up. My heart, my heart, he'd insisted. He was sitting up, still hooked to EKGs and not looking at me when he said, I have lived too long.

THE MOUNTAIN

People laughed. The king and queen laughed. The king and queen had us all laughing.

Then the little girl showed up.

The girl had walked from the mountain that blocked the view to the south. Limped, rather. She had limped all the way to where the people were laughing and had stood behind them, waiting. What was she doing back?

I was among the first to spot her, the first, in the midst of our disbelief and, I'd have to admit, first in my own series of chuckles, to step away.

There were no other children to hide among, to shield her from the stares of the people or to minimize the wrath of the royalty once they were apprised of her presence. That was the point: there were no other children, all the other children had run before her into the mountain because of him, his pretty pipe and song, and she, as slow as she was with that limp, was left behind, and hadn't made it into the mountain in time.

Or so she said.

We had all crawled and screed the sides and gulleys and peaks of that mountain until the price of rope rose on account of our having need of it, we had sonogrammed its side with jerry-built machines and laid stethoscopes the size of TV dishes against its stone heart and nothing, a big nothing was what we heard.

Except she said she heard more, she knew what was wanted.

The guy with the pipe and his song and the rats had wanted a lot. And the rats were all back in town inside a week. How were children like rats anyway? All we knew was that one Saturday the kids were whining, in our hair, and he played them a few numbers, and by dinner they were gone. And then this girl showed up with her story.

She had no parents to speak of, the man and woman accused of bearing her had long ago fled, so no one could defend her from the anger of the other parents, who hated her for the lameness that had spared her. In short, we beat her. If she wasn't a cripple before, she was well on her way now. The king and queen descended from their dais to intercede, slashing their scepter and crowns at the crowd with a more *Let us at her* than a *Take pity* flourish.

I admit it was hard to stop punching. Several, including myself, tried to throw a few into the air even while our arms were pinned back. But we listened closely when the king deigned to question her: The children are all dead? he asked the way you would, for confirmation.

No, no, they're fine, she said.

Fine? the king shouted, turning to us, trying to get us to shout our objections.

Pay up, she sighed.

Price. We had gone over this before. Around and around. I stepped forward with yet another *How much exactly?* Now I have only one child gone and not a gaggle like the Kennedys, like the Brady Bunches of steps and halves of children who went off wholesale behind the guy who had the pipe, so I suppose I'm not holding on to as much anger, if anger gets figured that way. I could still ask her what we could offer that was dearer than our very own children, how could we up that ante?

But I had the answer all along. I hid it as always while the others shrugged their shoulders or haggled, while the king and the queen slipped away to mount their carriage. It was always at the tip of my tongue. When I blurted it out, was I foolish? Perhaps.

It was, after all, the obvious.

The girl said, Go ahead, give it a try. There's that head of the pin, the eye of the needle problem, but no doubt that's just physics.

I would bring along a physicist.

But could we really manage without them was the question, the royalty I meant, not the children whom we could not hear, supposedly calling to us from inside of the mountain the way the girl said, reminding us of their lack of presence. The king and the queen wouldn't be really gone anyway, I argued, they would always be there for conducted tours and scenic drive-ups, although of course they understood the paying up had to be permanent.

Give them the king and queen.

The king and the queen hemmed and hawed. You could always have more children, they put forth, they laughingly suggested.

We laughed too, we nudged each other.

The little girl led us to the mountain and pounded on it with her cane. I think I have a deal, she shouted at the rock, Let me in. But before the rock of the mountain could roll itself back—what else?—two men, on a signal from the two with the crowns, dropped a rock on her head.

Since she made up our only link to the children, that was that. The king clapped me in chains and spent a bundle on having the whole incident forgotten. He ordered a bunch of signs with a circle around an X-ed out bouquet, big billboards covering up the mountain, and all the loud parents were either shipped to some Australia or made part of his cabinet where they could be watched and silenced with the usual privileges.

So they could laugh.

I spent a week chained to that mountain. I could actually hear something like children's voices now and then but by the time I'd gotten over my *No way,* they'd stopped. For myself, a week on the mountain was hard enough to get through. I must have been out of it to have heard anything. After they cut off those chains, I didn't talk voices, you'd better believe me. Not a word.

PINK PYRAMID

Glow is what they wait for. She unreels the transparent hose around the travel house and they wait until something comes up out of the ground to make it glow, so they can see at night, so they don't have to be like some extinct animal and go right to sleep after the sun sets. But that is what they do, they are so tired from traveling, the hose is so slow in working. She leans into his arm draped over their inflated travel furniture, and falls asleep.

She wakes to a space bright with what could be moonlight, except the moon is slim and dull. The hose, draped over the hooks around the room, is fully distended. Its pink light makes him look happy. But old. She is not that old but this kind of light bears down on every worn feature, every wind-blown pore, the lost hair. He has cropped what little of his hair is left into a tuft, like the plants back home he says he cares for as a volunteer. She admires that style of his, spikey yet nostalgic for the natural, and arranges the tuft into its place. He has fallen asleep with his hand in front of his face, hoping to see his hand in his dream as a way for his waking self to cross over. He is so much more interested in controlling his dreams than in being awake that they don't even make love before they sleep.

With the hose so bright, she sees the pyramid in the window through the shape of the absent stars. She slept in the pyramid's shadow all the time she worked on it, slept under the loose shell beside the plaques that were planted in the ground to explain how the mountain came to rise out of this level land. The debris was brought here over many years it said, until the pile rose so high no one could add to it without a mask to help them breathe. Then they gave up adding to the mountain, and began to shield it with shell. Not from those who would take glowing souvenir handfuls—they welcomed them—but to keep the mountain from crushing those souvenir-mongers. It became one of those forbidden, dangerous places that people like to visit to escape the crowds everywhere else, the crowds often so thick in the mornings you ended up pushed to the wrong place to work.

She remembers being happy working on the pyramid but now she thinks it might have been because the pinkness of the pyramid itself gave off well-being, the way the hose and the air do now. She and many of her fellow workers had lain under the shells at night to watch the stars under the looming pinkness and they were never tired or cross. They were pink.

Your night isn't usually this short, he says, sitting up. Why are you awake?

I'm hoping for more sleep, she says. But I can't get the hose unscrewed from the socket.

He can't either. Light will flood the room all night without the cutoff that neither of them can find. He helps her reel in the hose but the light is brighter under the tension of the storage spool. I hate these old places, he says. No one knows how they work anymore.

We used to build fires at night while we were working. When we needed to get more work finished and the hose took so long to glow.

I have never seen a fire, he says. Once, in my dreams.

You can't dream it without seeing it, she says. She tries pressing on the walls here and there but nothing opens, the seams resist her in her search for the cutoff. I am just doing this, if anyone asks, to make the house happy, she says. See, she says—they have it set for Happiness all right. She points at the arrow.

He can't help smiling but he turns his face into his arm again. Wake me, he says. If you find fire.

Now she wants to. That would gift him good, just once at least, to see it.

She begins to dig behind the house, through a hole someone's heel has left in the ground cover, and then through another. He couldn't know that she and the other workers had buried combustion containers here and there. They were made from the extinguishers sprayed constantly on the pyramid's innards, and on each other. Refilled with the pyramid's combustibles, they sold well off-site as fuel, heat and light, always clandestine. Once in a while, someone was caught smuggling the combustibles and then he was extinguished, rough justice, but not so often that the practice didn't flourish.

She used to bury the containers close to the surface, she used to just lay them in the ground and barely cover them over again so they would be easy to find. Squirreling they called it. Once someone dug deep and uncovered an unusually big one that no one remembered seeing, let alone burying. Instead of selling it, they ignited it themselves. How her eyes hurt after, the light was so bright. One of the workers lost his hand.

They called it an accident, so no one was extinguished.

Probably the small containers are all found since the travel house was put in but the idea of fire, even for a few minutes before someone catches her, is worth the trouble. They have to pay for every hole they put in anyway—that's what happened when you tore one open. Because nobody can walk anywhere without tearing through the ground cover, it is a good tax. Cheaper than having to pay for stepping on insects, which are so rare.

The first container she finds is broken, slit down the middle, its thin sides caved flat. Maybe she broke it herself, digging so hard. The second one she takes out of the hole as if it is one of those expensive insects, and thrusts it under her shirt as soon as she gets the dirt off, the way they used to. She doesn't worry about fire exploding at her chest. She won't live much longer anyway. Nobody has, who worked on the pyramid. *Pyre,* meaning *fire, mid,* meaning *measure.* Fire she understood, but measure? What did it measure? The lives of the workers? She leans forward to shield the container between her breasts, so no one can see it, at least in silhouette. Women are better at this than men. The loss of the container's weight from the earth will be known eventually by the sensors but not right away, not with sirens and the screeching of vehicles.

He is so involved with his dreams she is afraid if he sees the fire he will think he is dreaming. He does that with sex sometimes. He will be standing or sitting or lying beside her, hands all over her, but at the important moment he will close his eyes even tighter and something will happen that doesn't include her at all, and not his body either.

This is her challenge: she wants him to want her more than his dream. Maybe fire will help. They've only been together a few weeks, so she's not sure. They met at the border where travelers wait for partners. He wanted to see the pyramids to honor his people, old ones who made the mountain at the beginning so long ago. They had that in common, his ancestors and her work on it not so long ago. Together they made their way past the lean-tos hawking souvenir pyramids inside half-globes of pink dust to the entrance. The guards there offered patches to show you how long you should stay but they weren't really guards but cheap projections.

Surveillance is understood.

She has to hurry. He's awake again and soon he will have begun confusing being awake with dreaming. She trips on a hole she hasn't filled and lands on her face. The container hisses between her breasts. If she keeps her face away and hardly breathes—

She tries not to breathe but it's so hard, in her hurry, in her fear. She tries to pull in the darkness with her one breath, she tries to be the hose light. There's more darkness where she moves to so quickly.

She wedges the container upright in a hole in that darkness.

The light inside outlines him. He holds his hand in front of his face, palm away from his nose by an inch. It won't do to wait and show him later. Someone will find out and burn it himself. An old-fashioned container like this? It doesn't matter how few people are around here—fire is fire. She should bring it in and get credit for it. Instead, she blows at its nipple until it starts to smoke.

Maybe she will tell him he dreamt it anyway. Everything valuable happens in dream is what he believes. Fire will be hard to believe because his eyes will be so sore from watching his hand but still, a dream of it might make him happy too, happier than really seeing it. Since he began wanting to see that hand in his dream, he hasn't been happy. At least he faces the darkness she's in.

When the flames catch, he moves his hand away from his face. That's about how long the fire lasts. A good thing too, otherwise it would show up on the infrared. He could have smiled too but that she couldn't see, the sudden flare had blinded her.

She buries the burnt container as deep as she can, moving her hands fast. Then she smooths the surface, she pees on it so it will lose its roughness.

He's weeping when she goes inside. I wanted to touch it so much, he says.

You can't do that. She unrolls a tongue of food from the wall. Eat this, she says. It will calm you.

He looks at the food but he doesn't try it.

When I worked here, she tells him, fire came out of the mountain all the time, sometimes where we walked and sometimes after we placed the shell on the walls, in reaction to them. Once, in the early morning, one of us carrying a shell burst into flame. Those who hadn't seen fire yet thought she had wings. She wouldn't stop running until the flame came around her. No one could extinguish her quickly enough.

After that, she says, in a quieter tone—she had been very excited by the fire too, it lit up her memory of the place—gas escaped on one side, the last one we covered. All one day it hissed out. We could see it because we kept throwing green dye into it. At least we had the dye. The gas hurt our eyes, moved under our coverings. I have never seen so many people dancing in pain.

I've seen gas, he says. I was born near gas.

Nearly everyone is, she says. But not many can say they danced to it.

That's pretty strong, he says, and he takes a bite of the food. I saw my hand, he says.

She nods. Did it wave?

He can't be sure. The fire came just at the same time.

Once you see it, you'll see it again, she says.

I hope so, he says, looking at his hand.

Together they find a way to unscrew the hose light. It means they won't have light again but they don't care, its light is too much. They watch the dark in case someone has seen her, then, at the first sign of day, they go out into the open space near the pyramid and stand in it.

A caged bird calls out from one of the stalls in the pyramid's shadow. Its owner has a license to allow customers to listen to it. Of course the bird is lifelike but no one believes it's real. It's the same with the sound it makes: the *tweet, tweet* sounds mechanical. On the other hand, she says, at least it's nothing we've heard before and that's worth the fee.

My mother used to sing and it sounded nothing like that, he says. That sounded like something that's metal and turned too tight.

Crying, she says. That's how they do crying these days.

Why would a bird cry? They are watching the bird in projection diving into the horizon, eating other flying creatures out of the air, easing itself onto water. A bird had all of that, he says. It's hard to think it could be sad.

They leave the enclosure puzzled. A man nearby makes the same sound as the bird with his mouth, but only once. They have to pay him to repeat it. He covers his mouth when he performs so no one will know how he does it.

They walk away from the pyramid, so far that few sit nearby and that is where they make love. They could walk farther but the distance is about right—the pyramid disappears behind his prone side. It is hard to tell near the glare of the pyramid and the swirling pink everywhere, just who might be watching, who could watch. It is not easy to lose themselves in this act but he feels the bird should be celebrated, that part of them flies out when they excite each other. Did we cry or sing? he says when it's over.

She sneezes. They've raised a cloud of pink dust. There's a couple of other clouds in the distance but theirs is the thickest, the most recent. The dust coats her throat, the little hairs on her arms. She can see all the holes in the cover they'll have to pay for. We can't stay much longer, she says. They'll find out about the fire eventually.

We could starve for a while, he says, holding his hand up in the cloud, suspended in the dreamy light.

She nods. That's freedom for you. I can feel the hunger already, I've done it so often. She turns over on her stomach and hunches her head between her shoulders to avoid the slow-falling dust. I kind of like hunger.

He puts an arm around her and kisses her cheek. Time isn't everything. I mean, we could go back right now and just imagine staying on. We could dream it.

You and your dreams. It'll be really bad if I get so hungry I can't tell if I'm dreaming.

Hey, you could be dead, he says.

That's later, she says. Let's stay as long as we can.

He hadn't mentioned her death before. Border travelers often get stuck with someone who's about to die. Who else would want them? But those are the most adventurous, most exciting companions. You just have to be careful that the travelers are not projections, with so much energy they kill you instead.

She watches him lift his arms above his head, pumping them down, lifting them again. He gets up and runs in circles around her. *Tweet,* he calls out, he cries. Was that how they used birds for warning?

If the sky was falling, she says. Maybe he is projected is what she doesn't say. She's been wondering about that, he is so friendly. It is hard to tell without wind that would cause a projection to falter. It is a long way to get to wind.

I did hear about the sky falling, he says. But it didn't fall everywhere.

Some of the places must have had birds.

On their way back, they sight a pile of rocks lying on top of the land cover. He won't go near them but she does. Definitely rocks, she says. The kind they sell, although I don't see any advertising on them. He walks closer and she nudges one with her foot. He steps away. Probably someone left them here for a reason, he says. When I worked with plants, there was a big market for them.

Most of them don't last long, she says. Especially when they're like this, all together.

You are so stupid, he says. They could explode.

I wanted to show you how brave I am.

You made the fire last night. He backs away farther. But these scare me more.

She picks up one of the rocks. I could scare other people.

He looks all around. There's nobody even at the stalls in the heat of the day. But I suppose that's good, he says. You walk way ahead of me.

They walk with their heads down because the pyramid reflects the sun so well they are dazzled. It is very hard not to tear holes in the land cover walking like this, or to cover their steps. She moves quickly anyway, with the rock in her hand, expecting at any moment to fly apart. He catches up to her only after they round the pyramid's side and can see again. She throws the rock down then, right in front of him.

He screams.

It skips.

That's what I remember, she says. That's a rock.

He pounds his chest in fear but she can see he liked the thrill of not knowing if it would explode.

They are still standing there looking at the rock when a man passes them, carrying the empty birdcage. The door of the cage bangs where it hasn't been fastened. He slows down, seeing the rock. He's angry. Aren't you a little stupid to be playing with something like that?

She doesn't look at either man. She turns and walks away.

There were great armies, he says.

I'm sure, she says.

The sky and the land went dark with all the armies. The ocean's waves—

—were thick with them, she says. People fought each other everywhere. It's in the songs. More people dying than stars in the sky.

There are probably bones under our feet right now, he says, and shifts his clumsy feet over the land cover.

The few they didn't put in cemeteries to grind up? Maybe, she says. Her right arm is sore from leaning on it. She wishes for a chair, or even a pillow, she's flat to the ground. They can't go back to the place for their inflatables if they want to stay on and starve, it would be too conspicuous. She wonders why he's staying with her, he could find someone else to tour his old people's folly. They haven't been traveling that long.

He knows so much about his old people. He paces in the other direction but she can still hear him. History, he says. Over there—fifty thousand dead in two days. They had a lot of birds then, he says. They feasted. Somebody took a photograph that was saved, of the rest of the birds eating them later.

I wonder why that photograph, she says. Among all those other things. And who took it.

Or maybe nothing happened here at all, he says. Maybe they told the story about the picture just to make us feel good. That is very important, feeling good. There's no pink outside of storytelling to get that kind of feeling.

I would like to see that picture, just once, she says.

He turns away from her, his body pink from the sun, gray from the dirt. He rubs his hands across his thigh, dirtying it. I need a shower.

You haven't had enough of the pink then, she says. Take a deep breath.

He breathes in several times loudly, then says, Do you think that's rain over there?

She shakes her head at where he's pointing. Only if the cover's broken. You know, those bones will dissolve eventually. Were your people buried here?

People have been excavating pyramids for years, he says, and found little. Maybe not this one. He glances back at the stalls, where people crouch. People here fought over the price of something. Imagine—value had gotten that far out of control. We could probably find a few of the bones, something so small that no one's ground it up yet.

There were a lot of workers before me, even here.

He looks up at the sky. As far as you could see, they invaded. And there was none of this cover. People could walk anywhere your feet could put you. He almost scuffs the ground cover.

He is beginning to see all the people here, old ones too. It bothers her. She starts walking again. That's got to be food, she says. A ridge that looks like that means food.

It's so far away, it could be anything. He's a few steps behind her. But we're starving, right?

They walk toward the ridge anyway. It's a direction.

I am so thirsty, she says. That's what always gets me in the end. It's not the eating.

Feel that?

She puts out her hand. Yeah. If you walk fast enough, you feel something like wind. You've never felt that before?

I never had the space to walk so far. He wiggles his hand, lifts it over his head.

It's the bones in the ground, she says. They pull at your hand.

He laughs at her. You think I'm a projection?

You could be.

What difference would it make?

She's not sure. She's dying.

Well, I can't wait any longer anyway, he says. I'll prove it to you. He leaves his waste in a pile. Carefully—she helps too—they fit it under the land cover and smooth it down.

You shouldn't have eaten so much before starving.

He slaps his belly.

They watch steam rise from pyramid. It does that now and then. No one knows when to avoid it, she tells him.

He starts to move away. Pink, pink, pink, he says. He walks far ahead of her until he stops and finds a tear in a corner of the land cover. Dig here.

That's only a legend. A thousand years ago, maybe.

Try. It can't hurt. We've already walked all over the place and torn up more land cover than either of us can afford.

She kneels and pulls the cover toward her, piling dirt on the land next to her. It shouldn't be very far down. That's what they say.

There's sand underneath here so there has to be something.

If water were easier, nobody would ever even try this, she says, sweating, digging.

The ground does get damp. She shoves her fist into it and turns her hand to palm the moisture, she licks at the pinkness she brings up while he takes over her digging. You'll see your hand for sure tonight, she says.

He's gasping, digging, the hole's about as deep as they can get it without getting into it. They lay their tongues on the cool wet pink but it is hard to tell whether the ground absorbs their moisture or they take it from the ground.

Kind of sweet, he says, wiping the dirt out of his mouth. As usual.

She rests on her heels. Let's go. We shouldn't stay this long.

They refill the hole quickly. It's not so hot when they start out again, it's that much later.

Tell me about the gentlemen's war, she says.

I've only heard a little, he says. Everyone worked so hard that in every aspect of their lives they had other people take over the experience part of things. You know, someone else did the eating, someone else kissed the children, someone else found missing papers. These gentlemen, as they were called, met once a year to exchange what experiences they did have. But they fouled up.

That's not so hard to do. After all, someone else probably did it for them.

They were peculiar about their experiences. They wanted to have them and not have them at the same time so when they had to do the exchange everyone had to be in on it. Anyway, there was some confusion and all the experiences were accidentally destroyed.

How could that happen? Didn't they have them saved with electronics?

It wasn't the way it is now, with electronics controlling even the wind, and the turning of the Earth. It was wilder. You could turn the electronics off and on then. The current wasn't as strong.

I can't imagine, she says.

The gentlemen got themselves turned off. They went on alone. And that's it, that's all I know. Even I can't see them when I dream. Unless, he says, stopping, they are having my dreams.

You have seen your hand, right?

I have.

This proves they are your dreams, not any gentleman's.

He looks at his hand. It could have been someone else's hand, he says.

A projected hand?

He laughs but he looks around. I've never been alone like this before.

It isn't that dangerous, she says, slowing a little. Lots of people take a few days here and there, they fast and come back.

I've always wanted to.

Not everybody likes it.

Not everybody sees fire, he says. He says he heard somebody ask about extra light from last night where they visited the bird.

You're just telling me now? she says.

For a while the sum zero will be the same for the area. We aren't set to cross any borders for a day or so. No one would think we are even starving the way we're going now, he says. A projection, maybe.

She checks around. No cloud, no figure, just the pink pyramid in the southern corner and the sun at an angle, all the steam gone, and pink.

I was watching, he says. No one followed us.

It's not as if we couldn't figure out fire all by ourselves, she says. What are they afraid of?

You worked on the pyramid, you're the expert. There's not much more that can be controlled. Not really. I love the blankness here.

I don't know about love. Here's food, she says, stumbling up to the ridge with its tongue. They don't eat it though. Without water, it is too hard to swallow. And don't they want to starve another day?

After dark comes and he has already curled up with his hand in front of him and is sleeping, she spots another fire. Sometimes when she blinks, the fire's not there afterwards. Maybe it's the reflection of something very bright from somewhere that's still under the sun. She's heard of buildings that high but she hasn't seen one. She can't resist walking toward it.

Her leaving wakes him and he catches up with her. Seeing one fire attracted another, he says.

This is not a dream, she says but he doesn't really hear her, he is hurrying to get to the fire, to see it again on his own.

They are soon enough holding their hands in front of it. Can you see my bones in my hand through the light?

Yes, she says. But she's watching the two skeletal figures tending the fire come closer. They have made their mouths look kind, and they offer water. There's a border past the smoke, they warn them. Stay away from the border.

Smoke? He has never seen smoke. The fire the night before had been too fast. He steps toward a drift of it and backs away. Not like steam.

Beautiful, she says.

The male thanks her. We made it yesterday, he says. They will fine us today for sure. You'd better not stay.

We're starving too.

All four of them watch the fire lick. It likes the land cover and the wind is pushing the fire away from them, into other land cover, the fire is catching. Someone will see it soon.

She pulls his hand into the smoke and he watches the smoke cover and uncover it, he blinks, he closes his eyes, he sniffs as his hand keeps disappearing. It's real, he says.

The skeletal couple shows them how to dig a bed under the land cover so they can't be seen. In the morning, you fill the bed in and move away fast, before the tax comes, the female tells them. But remember the salt in the dirt will sting you.

This is when she sees that salt has eaten the male's skin in one of his bony corners, made it pink and raw.

The pyramid area isn't large even if you fast and walk as far as you can away from it all day to where the border lies and others wait, their inflatables in balls beside them. You always see the pyramid, there is no real escape. Halfway back they pass a woman with a birthing belly who's waddling toward the smoke.

She hasn't thought of the baby since she left here, the thought glows inside her but wordless, an ache.

They take a seat on a stretch of raised land cover. The pyramid is right behind them. They both avoid looking toward the border, so they see the insect at the same time. It escapes the land cover through some tear of theirs, some costly tear.

Its shell resembles the pyramid's, she says.

Look at its legs go! he says. It's really alive!

It could be just circuits, she says. Or a projection.

No, they fix the dirt, he says.

That's what they say, she says. I don't believe them. I am going to eat it.

She is quick enough. Its taste is pure pink. She tells him that and they know the cost of that taste, they are both quiet, then she feels along the side of the pyramid that is so hot she can't really touch it until—

Here is the baby.

The mouth looks like just another whorl of stone, the skin as dark as what's packed around her. They touch the shiny hot facing with their fingers. Nobody but she would know where to find her, she tells him. The baby was green anyway, she says.

He nods. Sometimes they last.

Not around here. She lets go.

He catches her before she hits the ground. She writhes in his arms then stops, then he loads her on his back. It's a long way to where he has to take her and of course she's heavy, and heavier walking across the land, the white sun in his wet eyes.

His tears surprise him. He had assumed there wasn't enough liquid in his body to produce them. He tries to catch them with his tongue but his tongue dries in the air instead, his tongue lies heavy in his head, heavier than her body. But he likes to carry her despite her weight and how hard it is for him to walk. She feels familiar even this way, but slowly she becomes less familiar, becomes a burden. He lays her down on the earth covering, he kind of collapses under her. There is no hurry.

He's always wondered why the area for bodies is so warm and he suspects it has to do with fire, now that he's seen it. He wants so much to have to do with fire. Some live for lightning, some for the wind coming out of the N-N-W, or smoke. He wants to wildcat fire in the future, he wants it on his hands, he wants to trade it. All his grief is fire.

She never bothered to wear a suit like the others when she worked here. She lasted just as long. She showed him fire. And the baby.

He fashions her below-hair into curls and gives her up to this warm place. The entrance is like any other, a lip out of the ground that opens to the right number, which is given to him by a machine after it reads her pulse, her pulselessness. Is it a dream? Does he throw himself in after her at the moment the lip opens, or does the heat suck him in? He can't resist the sudden bright flames.

ACKNOWLEDGMENTS

"Hot Rain" in GRANTA

"Alfalfa" in EPIPHANY, reprinted in LITHUB

"Mugsy" in WIGLEAF

"Camp Clovis" and "Endangered Species" in PRAIRIE
SCHOONER

"Bomb Jockey" in ONE STORY

"Cordless in the Fifties" and "All Mapped Out" in MISSIS-
SIPPI REVIEW

"Dirty Thirties" in NUMERO CINQ

"Ogallala Aquifer" in CHICAGO TRIBUNE

"Pink Pyramid" in CONJUNCTIONS

"Mennonite Forest" in MASSACHUSETTS REVIEW

"Africa" in NARRATIVE

"The Mountain" in WITNESS

Parts of "Hot Rain" appeared as "A Thankful Scenario" in
BLACKBIRD

I'm very grateful for all the valuable comments by Molly
Giles, Gay Walley, and Steve Bull, and for the environmental
reports shared by the brilliant activist Susan Henderson about

the Black Hills Army Depot, and the intrepid *Grant Tribune* reporter who followed the story in Nebraska so long ago. Thank you Margaret Sutherland Brown for your thoughtful edits, agenting, and enthusiasm. Thanks also to all at the Floyd Memorial Library and to Yaddo; MacDowell; Bogliasco Foundation; The Bellagio Center; the James Merrill House; Ossabaw Island Foundation; Hawthornden Castle; Swan's Island Lighthouse; the House of Translation in Paros, Greece; Virginia Center for the Creative Arts, where I have worked; and the generosity of a New York Foundation for the Arts Fellowship and a fellowship to the Sewanee Writing Conference.

In memory of William Melvin Kelley, Sondra Spatt Olson, and Larry Orsak, entomologist extraordinaire.

To Dad, of course, who is not a memory.